"What brought you out here this morning, *Deputy* Jennings?"

She emphasized his title, as if it were a bad thing. "Did your sister talk to you?"

He cleared his throat then walked over to the railing and leaned back on it, so that they were almost back-to-back. He turned his head to study her serious profile. It was as if she didn't want to make eye contact. "It's not what you think. My sister always respects doctor-patient confidentiality."

"But you suspected something more was going on than a rock through a church window?"

Nick let the silence stretch between them. A gust of wind rustled up and bent the cornstalks growing in the fields next to her house.

Sarah ran a hand down her long ponytail and shifted to face him, a serious expression in her bright blue eyes. "I'm afraid he's found me."

Alison Stone lives with her husband of more than twenty years and their four children in Western New York. Besides writing, Alison keeps busy volunteering at her children's schools, driving her girls to dance and watching her boys race motocross. Alison loves to hear from her readers at Alison@AlisonStone.com. For more information please visit her website, alisonstone.com. She's also chatty on Twitter, @alison_stone. Find her on Facebook at Facebook.com/alisonstoneauthor.

Books by Alison Stone

Love Inspired Suspense

Plain Pursuit
Critical Diagnosis
Silver Lake Secrets
Plain Peril
High-Risk Homecoming
Plain Threats
Plain Protector

PLAIN PROTECTOR

ALISON STONE

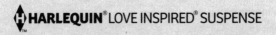

HARLEQUIN® LOVE INSPIRED® SUSPENSE

Recycling programs
for this product may
not exist in your area.

LOVE INSPIRED BOOKS

ISBN-13: 978-0-373-67752-8

Plain Protector

www.Harlequin.com

Printed in U.S.A.

But when I am afraid, I will put my trust in You.
—Psalms 56:3

To my daughter Kelsey. You are smart, kind and beautiful. You work hard to reach your goals, yet take everything in stride. This ability amazes me and will take you far in life. I am so proud of you. I love you.

And to Scott, Scotty, Alex and Leah.
Love you guys, always and forever.

ONE

Sarah Gardner never thought a master's degree in social work would mean she'd be sweeping the floor of the basement meeting room of the Apple Creek Community Church on a Sunday evening. No, she had thought she'd have her own office in a hospital or a private clinic, a family and maybe even a child by now.

But when Sarah was a promising young college student, she couldn't imagine the things her life would be lacking at the ripe old age of thirty. No decent job, no car, no close friends. All in an effort to maintain a low profile for fear her ex-boyfriend would find her.

Yes, her life was a mess because she'd chosen the wrong guy to date. She swept a little more vigorously than necessary, sending a cloud of dust into the air, making her cough.

A loud slam made Sarah jump. She spun around to find Mary Ruth Beiler with her hand on the closet door and an apologetic look on her face. Sometimes Sarah envied the young Amish girl who seemed to have her entire life mapped out for her in the insular Amish community of Apple Creek, New York. Mary Ruth's options had been pruned to the point that she didn't have much room to make bad choices.

But not having choices didn't mean freedom. Sarah knew as much.

"Sarah," Mary Ruth said in a soft voice, "I put the folding chairs in the closet. Is there anything else you need help with before I go?"

"I think we're set." Sarah wanted to make a few notes from the group meeting tonight before her thoughts slipped away, much like the wisps of dreams from her childhood that vanished when she opened her eyes after a fitful night's sleep.

Sarah had set up a group meeting for primarily Amish youth, whose parents would rather they be attending the Sunday evening singings. But holding the meeting the same night as the bimonthly Sunday singings gave the teens an excuse to leave home without explaining where they were heading. They came to discuss the dangers of drinking and drugs—for some a reality, for others merely a temptation—and other worldly concerns. Sarah suspected some of their parents knew where their sons and daughters were really going and only pretended their offspring were enjoying the singings with hopes that soon they would be back within the fold. Other parents flat out forbade their children from associating with this *Englischer* who was surely giving them worldly ideas.

But if these same Amish parents knew the trouble their precious children were flirting with, they might remember Sarah in their prayers instead of regarding the outsider with a sideways glance and a cold shoulder.

Lord knew she could use their prayers.

"Yes, we're all set," Sarah said. "Thank you for your help." She dug into her jeans' pocket and handed the girl payment, payment she could ill afford if she had to remain holed up in Apple Creek much longer like she was some criminal on the run and not the victim that she was. The pastor of the church paid her a modest stipend to work with the youth in the community.

Having sweet Mary Ruth as an assistant was a bridge, however precarious, to the Amish youth, many of whom needed Sarah's services, but, like their parents, were leery of outsiders. Some kids had found their way to drugs and alcohol— just like the youth she used to work with back in Buffalo—and their peers knew it. Mary Ruth made the first few introductions. From there, word spread. The rumor mill among the teens in Amish country was no less efficient than their texting counterparts in the outside world.

Now, every two weeks, Mary Ruth helped Sarah set up the room and serve as a friendly face to newcomers and repeat visitors alike. The gatherings usually only had four or five members, but even if she only touched one person's life, it would be worth the effort.

Most Sundays, Mary Ruth then ran off to the Sunday singings. But not this week. This week she had stayed, a part of the group but separate. She seemed intrigued by the choices some of her peers had made, or choices they were courting.

Sarah hoped the youth kept her number one rule: what was said in this room, stayed in this room. She trusted Mary Ruth, but each newcomer was a risk. Despite their age difference, Sarah considered Mary Ruth a friend.

Perhaps her only friend in Apple Creek.

"Do you need my help at all during the week?" Mary Ruth lingered at the stairway leading to the exit.

"Yes, if you'd like. I was going to make a few home visits to young, single mothers in town who might be in need of services." The women weren't Amish and often needed help understanding what services were available to them and their babies until they got back on their feet.

"These new mothers really need you, don't

they?" Mary Ruth asked, as if she were just now coming to appreciate Sarah's work in the community.

"Some of them don't have anyone else."

"It's sad. Their future is uncertain." Mary Ruth played with the folds in her long dress, its hem brushing the tops of her black boots.

The irony that Sarah's future was probably the most precarious of them all was not lost on her, but she kept her thoughts to herself.

"I admire the work you do. Sometimes I wish Amish women could be independent like you."

Independent. Sarah outwardly appeared independent, but on the inside she was a trembling mess. "How old are you, Mary Ruth?"

"Eighteen?" Her answer sounded more like a question.

"Ah, you have your whole life in front of you."

"A life that has already been planned out." There was a faraway quality to her voice. "Most of my friends are hoping to get married soon."

"And you?"

Mary Ruth hitched a shoulder and her cheeks turned pink. The Amish didn't talk much about dating and courtship, at least not to her. Some successfully hid their wedding plans until the church published their engagement announcement only weeks before their actual wedding.

Sarah did know that Mary Ruth had been

spending time with a young Amish man, Ruben Zook, who lived next door to the cottage Sarah rented. But she didn't dare inquire about Mary Ruth's plans, respecting the Amish ways.

Sarah waved her hand. "You're a smart girl. I'm sure you'll figure it out."

"Guten nacht," Mary Ruth said, in a singsong voice as she climbed the stairs, her mood seeming to lift. She very rarely spoke Pennsylvania Dutch to Sarah, except for when she said good-night. Sarah was still smiling when the outside door opened with a creak and then slammed shut.

Unease whispered at the back of Sarah's neck as a pronounced silence settled across the room. Her plan to sit at her desk in her tiny basement office and make notes no longer seemed like a smart idea. It had been a habit during her years of working in Buffalo. Make notes immediately so that one patient didn't blend in with the next. However, here in Apple Creek, her workload was lighter and she had no distractions at home.

Here, she didn't have a boyfriend pestering her to know what she was doing every minute of every day. Nor did she have to worry that she'd inadvertently provide the wrong answer. An answer that would send him into a blind rage.

Icy dread pooled in the pit of her stomach. *How did I allow myself to get tangled up with*

Jimmy Braeden? She had always considered herself a smart girl.

Even smart girls made bad choices sometimes.

Letting out a long breath and wishing she could silence all the doubts and worries in her head, Sarah gathered up her papers and jammed them into her bag with shaky hands. She hated that Jimmy had made her afraid. Made her hide. Made her into someone even she couldn't heal.

A shadow crossed the basement floor and Sarah glanced up at the narrow windows that faced the church parking lot. Nothing. Just the fading blue sky, which made her realize if she didn't hurry, she'd have to walk the mile home in the dark.

Sure, Jimmy didn't know where she was. *She hoped.* But that didn't mean it was wise to tempt fate as a single woman alone after dark on a deserted country road.

Sarah hoisted the strap of her bag over her shoulder and flipped off the light switch at the bottom of the stairs when a crashing sound exploded, disrupting the quiet night air. Shards of glass rained down over her head.

Sarah bit back a yelp and flattened herself against the wall of the basement under the broken window. Her pulse beat wildly in her ears as she fumbled in her bag. She was searching for a cell phone, when she remembered she didn't have one. It was one of the many things she had given up when she decided to disappear.

A cell phone was too easy to trace.

Sarah gingerly touched her head and her fingers came back sticky. She closed her eyes and muttered a silent prayer: *Dear Lord, please protect me.* If there was one thing she clung to through her turned-upside-down life, it was her faith. One constant in a crazy world.

Biting her lip, she glanced toward the stairs. Toward the exit. The unlocked door. Dread knotted her stomach. She stood, frozen, until her heart rate returned to normal. *Almost.* She figured her nerves wouldn't truly settle until she was safely at home, locked inside.

Her gaze landed on a large rock in the center of the room. Good thing she hadn't been struck by that or she might be unconscious.

Sarah couldn't stand here forever. She took a hesitant step toward the stairs.

Was someone waiting for her outside?

With a burst of courage—the same courage that had her leave her abusive ex—Sarah bolted up the stairs, clinging to her bag as if it could protect her. She pushed the door open and the still night air greeted her. Without a backward glance, she bolted as fast as her legs would carry her across the wide expanse of the parking lot to the pastor's house on the opposite side.

She pounded up the porch steps and lifted her fist and hammered on the door, immediately taking her back to another day, another time, when her boyfriend was chasing her. Promising he'd kill her if he caught her. Swallowing her dizzying panic, she glanced over her shoulder.

No one was chasing her now.

Just the shadows. And the haunting memories that refused to leave her alone.

When Deputy Sheriff Nick Jennings pulled up in front of the Apple Creek Diner, he had only two things on his mind: coffee and Flo's pie. His stomach growled as he considered his options. He was in the mood for some banana cream. As he pulled the door's release, his radio crackled to life. He listened intently, frowning when he heard there had been an incident at the church. Flo's pie would have to wait.

"I'm at the Apple Creek Diner," he said into the radio. "I can be at the church in three minutes." Nick flipped on the lights and pressed his foot to the floor, not necessary since he was only a few minutes out, but he missed the occasional adrenaline surge. Policing small-town Apple Creek didn't provide the same rush as serving in the army in times of war.

Not that he wanted to go back to war.

"The victim, a Miss Sarah Lynn, is at the pastor's residence," the dispatcher said. "The pastor's wife claims she's pretty shaken up."

Sarah Lynn? The name didn't register.

Nick tightened his grip on the steering wheel and as promised, made it to the parking lot of the church in under three minutes. Dusk had cloaked the area in the first hint of shadows, and his headlights arched across two people standing on the pastor's stoop. One was Miss Ellinor, the pastor's wife, the other was a petite woman he had noticed around town. That must be Sarah Lynn.

Nick had only been back in Apple Creek for a few months himself when this young woman arrived. Residents of a small town tended to notice new arrivals, even if they weren't petite and pretty, which this one certainly was. Flo at the diner, who had a habit of trying to fix him up, mentioned that this woman seemed to keep to herself most of the time, hadn't even offered up her name. A few speculated on why she had suddenly shown up in town—employment, low rent or maybe she was hiding from something— but mostly the residents of Apple Creek let her be. Nick assumed she probably did have her share of secrets. Having come off a bad breakup with a woman who was a master secret keeper, Nick figured he'd pass.

Nick climbed out of his cruiser and strode toward the pastor's neat, white-sided home. He tipped his hat toward the women. "Hello, Miss Ellinor." He thought it best if he waited for the young woman to introduce herself. That's when he noticed she was doing more than touching her forehead, she was holding a cloth to it.

"Are you injured?"

"I'm fine. My name is Sarah. Sarah Lynn…" The corners of her mouth turned down and the woman seemed to be studying her shoes. This woman was either afraid or hiding something. Perhaps both.

Apparently the residents of Apple Creek were collectively a pretty good judge of character.

"I'm Deputy Sheriff Nick Jennings. What happened here?"

Sarah shook her head, but it was Miss Ellinor who spoke first. "Someone smashed one of the basement windows of the church. I'm afraid Sarah has a pretty deep cut on her forehead. You'll probably have to call an ambulance. Is an ambulance coming?"

Sarah held up her hand, her eyes growing wide. "I don't need an ambulance. I'm fine." Her voice shook. She didn't sound fine.

"May I take a look?" Nick stepped toward

Sarah and she took a half step back, hemmed in by the front door of the pastor's home behind her.

Sarah dropped her hand and her long hair fell over the wound. She stared up at him with a look of defiance, although he may have misinterpreted the emotion in the dim lighting.

Nick held up his hands in a nonthreatening gesture. "I don't need to look at it, but *someone* should."

"I'm fine, really." Sarah's repeated use of the word *fine* seemed forced. She bent and picked up a heavy-looking bag. When she straightened, all the color drained from her face. If he hadn't been watching her, he might not have seen the terror that flashed across her pretty features and then disappeared into the firm set of her mouth and her narrowed gaze.

He wasn't going to have her pass out on his watch. "Let me drive you to the hospital. Have someone take a look at that cut."

Sarah pressed the wadded-up paper towel to her forehead and frowned. "I'm fine, really." There was that word again. "I just want to go home."

Miss Ellinor's features grew pinched. "Child, I know you like to put on a brave face, but if you don't get that cut checked out, you're going to end up with a big scar on your forehead. It would be a shame to mar that pretty face of yours. Wouldn't you agree, Deputy Jennings?"

Nick felt a corner of his mouth tugging into a grin, despite suspecting his amusement might annoy the young woman. Miss Ellinor, the pastor's wife, was a chatty soul who said whatever was on her mind. Being a woman of a certain age and position, no one seemed to call her on it. "A scar on that pretty face would be a shame."

Sarah squared her shoulders, apparently unsure of how to take his compliment.

Nick tipped his head toward his patrol vehicle. "I'll take you to the emergency room."

"Is this really necessary?" Sarah skirted past him and clearly had no intention of getting into his car.

"Would you rather I call an ambulance?"

Sarah sighed heavily. "I do *not* need an ambulance."

Nick decided to change his line of questioning. "Any idea who might have tossed a rock through the window?"

Miss Ellinor shook her head. "Bored kids causing trouble, I suppose."

Nick thought he noticed Sarah blanch. "I'm a social worker, and every other Sunday, to coincide with the Amish Sunday-night singings, I run a group meeting for Amish youth who may have alcohol or drug issues. Or other concerns."

"Really?"

Sarah slowly turned, her sneaker pivoting on the gravel. "Is there something wrong with that? This community is an underserved area. For some Amish youth, the years leading up to their baptism can be stressful. It's a huge decision, which can lead to unhealthy behaviors to deal with stress. Because of their insular life, they are often ill equipped to handle the temptation of drugs and alcohol." Despite the cool bite to her tone, she sounded rehearsed, like she was reading from a brochure.

"No, ma'am. I didn't mean to imply that what you're doing is wrong. Do you have reason to believe someone from your meeting tonight took issue with you? Or something that was said?"

Sarah adjusted the paper towel on her forehead. "I'm a social worker. Unfortunately, being…" she seemed to be searching for the right word "…*harassed* on occasion is one of the challenges of the job." She cut her gaze toward him, making a show of running her eyes the length of his deputy sheriff's uniform. "You can understand that." Unfortunately, in today's climate, he could.

"I'm issued a gun. What do you have for protection?" His pulse ticked in his jaw, anger growing in his gut. If some punk was messing with a social worker who was trying to help him, Nick would have to set him straight.

"Oh my, we've never had trouble here before." Miss Ellinor's hands fluttered at the collar of her floral shirt. Her white hair seemed to glow under the bright porch light.

Sarah reached for Miss Ellinor's hand and squeezed it. "It's okay. I wouldn't know what to do with a gun. And," she said, lowering her voice, "I don't think someone would be receptive to my help if I had a gun strapped to my body."

"Any self-defense classes then?" Nick didn't understand why he was so interested in this woman. He was here to answer a call about a broken window. See that she receive medical attention. That's it.

"I took a few self-defense classes back when I was in college. But, I do my best to avoid conflict. Beats getting my head trapped in a head-lock." Half her mouth quirked up. Nick could tell she was trying to defuse the situation with humor, but what happened here tonight wasn't funny.

Sarah cleared her throat and pulled the paper towel away from her forehead and suddenly seemed impatient to leave.

"Wait by the vehicle. I need to check out the broken window. I won't be but a minute."

Sarah nodded.

"Make sure she gets that cut looked at, Nick," Miss Ellinor hollered after him.

He waved and smiled. "Sure thing." He had a feeling that was going to be a difficult promise to keep.

Nick checked out the broken window, then went inside and assessed the damage. A large rock sat in the middle of the room. *Punks.*

When he returned to his vehicle, he found Sarah standing alone. "Miss Ellinor had to go in. She's babysitting her granddaughter. The pastor's not home. I told her I'd clean up the mess tomorrow."

Nick nodded, but didn't say anything. Sarah looked tiny standing next to his cruiser, one hand pressed to her forehead, the other arm wrapped around her middle. A large bag resting on her hip. He opened his passenger door and she cut him a cynical gaze. "Not going to make me ride in the back?"

"Are you a criminal?" He arched an eyebrow.

Without answering, she slipped into his car. "I'm not going to the hospital. You can take me directly home."

Despite Sarah's firm tone, her hands shook under the dome light as she fastened her seatbelt. She looked like a deer frozen in headlights, uncertain if safety existed a few steps away or if annihilation under the massive weight of an eighteen wheeler bearing down on her was inevitable.

The familiar sight of the interior of the patrol vehicle, with all its lights, displays and gadgets made Sarah suck in a breath, only to inhale the distinct police-car smell: part antiseptic, part vinyl, part whoever had been transported in the backseat. And the crackle of the radio sent Sarah reeling back to another time.

Sarah threaded her trembling hands, trying to maintain her composure. Trying to stay in the here and now. *I will not have a panic attack. I will not give this man a reason to question me any more than he already has. I can do this.*

Breathe...

"Any idea which of your clients could have thrown a rock through the church window? Anyone particularly angry or rude this evening?"

Sarah shook her head, not trusting her voice. "I'd just be guessing." *Or lying.* Did she really believe it was one of the Amish men or women from her meeting tonight? "If you don't mind, I'm tired. Can you please take me home?"

"I promised Miss Ellinor I'd get that cut on your head looked after. I'm not a man who goes back on a promise."

Sarah sighed heavily. She wasn't up for all this chivalrous stuff. She had been conned by the biggest con man himself, and she didn't trust herself when it came to reading people's—no, scratch that—men's true intentions.

Act tougher than you are. Don't let him take control.

Sarah shifted in her seat and squared her shoulders. "Truth be told, I don't have any insurance, and as you might have guessed, living in Apple Creek, working as a social worker, I'm not in a position to be forking out money for unnecessary medical expenses. As it is, I'll have a tough time paying my rent this month." She figured God would forgive her this little lie. She did have medical insurance, but she didn't dare use it. Just one more way for her former boyfriend to track her down. Everything she had Googled about vanishing had said to wipe her digital blueprint clean.

In today's modern world, that was tougher than ever.

Checking into a hospital with all the paperwork and computer records would likely raise a red flag if her former boyfriend was still looking for her. *If.* Inwardly she rolled her eyes. Of course he was still looking for her. Jimmy Braeden didn't give up a fight easily.

Sarah turned her head slowly, keenly aware

of the man studying her in the confined space of his patrol vehicle. Her heartbeat kicked up a notch, but surprisingly not out of fear, but out of uncertainty. How was she going to convince him to take her home?

She forced a smile. "Please, take me home." She tried once again for the direct approach.

He smiled back, revealing perfectly even white teeth. "I can't do that." Under other circumstances, Sarah would have immediately put up her defenses. She had vowed she'd never let a man control her like Jimmy had. Yet, Deputy Jennings seemed to give off a different vibe than her macho ex. There was something soft around his hard edges.

But her hunches had been wrong before. Just the fact that she was in this situation proved her point. She couldn't let her guard down because a handsome man smiled at her.

"I have a place I can take you." Deputy Jennings shifted the vehicle into drive and her stomach lurched.

"No, please. Take me home."

He cut her a sideways glance and his eyebrow twitched. Had he sensed her growing panic? If he had, he didn't say as much.

"You can call me Nick."

"*Nick*, take me home." Frustration bubbled up inside her. The thought of pulling the door handle while they cruised at forty-five miles per hour down the country road entered her mind and left just as quickly. She had tried that once before, and Jimmy had grabbed her ponytail and yanked her back in, promising he'd snap her neck if she ever tried that again.

Nick didn't look like the kind of man who would lay a hand on a woman.

Jimmy didn't look like that kind of man, either. Not initially.

"Please, I need to go home."

A look of confusion flickered across Nick's face before he focused on the road in front of him again. "It's okay. I won't take you to the hospital. My sister runs a small health-care clinic on the edge of town. It won't cost you anything. If we hurry, we can catch her before she closes up for the night. She usually works late. She can stitch you up right quick."

When Sarah gasped, Nick added, "It won't be bad, I've had plenty of stitches over the years, much to the dismay of my nanny. My sister'll do it as a favor to me. Don't worry about the cost."

"Oh, I can't." Sarah's head throbbed. She really, *really* wanted to go home and forget this miserable day. She couldn't take free services that were meant for someone who really needed them. And they'd ask for her name. Details that could get her killed.

Her anxiety spiked. If she freaked out now, Deputy Jennings—Nick—would think she had a screw loose. Best to remain calm and not raise any more suspicions.

The yellow dash on the country road mesmerized Sarah. She had gotten used to hoofing it these past six months. A car required a license, registration, a digital footprint. Again, all things that would reveal her location, only sixty miles away from her stalker. She'd run away, but not too far. She needed to be able to reach her sick mother in Buffalo in an emergency. But for now, she stayed away, prayed for her mother's health and maintained a low profile.

"How come we've never officially met before?" Nick asked, as if reading her thoughts.

"I haven't been in town long." *Be vague.*

"What brought you to Apple Creek?" He cut a sideways glance before returning his attention to what was in front of him and the equally spaced cat's eyes dotting the edge of the dark road. His question sounded innocent enough, but how could she be sure?

"I'm a social worker working with individuals who are either addicted or susceptible to drug or alcohol addiction. I also work with single mothers—not necessarily Amish—to help them access programs and—"

"You mentioned that before. But why here?

Why Apple Creek?" Nick glanced at her quickly, then back at the road.

"Why not?" Her words came out clipped despite her efforts to keep her tone even.

"Seems like a remote place. Most newcomers to Apple Creek nowadays are the Amish folk. Do you have ties to the area? Family?"

She crossed her ankles, then uncrossed them when she thought about the possibility of being in an accident and having her legs pinned against the dash in a contorted position. Sarah had a knack for worrying about everything.

She cleared her throat. "The Amish are an underserved area. Many young adults are afraid to reveal their problems, substance abuse or otherwise, to their own community for fear of punishment from the church. At least with me, I can help them work through their issues without the added burden of feeling like they've let down their parents or the church. My hope is to help my clients be the best person they can be, whether they decide to stay in the community or not. No judgment on my part."

"How does that go over with the Amish community?" His tone reminded her of when people asked, "How's that working for ya?" when it obviously wasn't working at all.

"I want to believe most Amish people appreciate my efforts, even if they won't publicly acknowledge what I'm doing. I can respect that. The Amish are a humble people who prefer to remain true to their own community." She wanted, no she *needed*, to work under the radar. Nick didn't need to know that. The fewer people who knew her predicament, the less likely she'd be discovered. "If I can help someone who is struggling with drugs or alcohol, everyone benefits." Sarah let out a long sigh. Her own father had been killed by a drunk driver. Sarah had heard more than once that social workers tended to come out of the ranks of individuals who needed some fixing in their own lives. If only the person who'd decided to drink and drive the day her father had been killed had chosen a different path. Had chosen to get help. How different her life might have been.

"Do you think the person who threw the rock tonight was someone from your group meeting? Or maybe an angry family member who doesn't appreciate what they might consider outside interference?"

"I don't want to believe one of the people I'm trying to help did this." A chill skittered up her spine. *Actually, Deputy Jennings, I think it was my crazy ex-boyfriend, but I don't know how he would have found me.* Sarah had taken tremendous pains to keep her location secret. The only ones who knew her background were the pastor and his wife. And Sarah trusted them completely.

Of course, her mom back in Buffalo knew where her daughter was, but was careful to only contact her through her pastor, who would relay the message to Pastor Mike here in Apple Creek.

Sarah's life had become a tangled web of carefully crafted half-truths and secrets. The more she talked, the greater chance she had of being discovered. That's why outside of work she had primarily kept to herself since she arrived in Apple Creek six months ago.

"Most of my clients' names are kept confidential." Even as the words slipped from her mouth, she knew that wasn't foolproof for confidentiality. Trust was the foundation of her group meetings. She couldn't control what clients revealed about themselves or others once they left.

Being a social worker, regardless of the community, had inherent risks: unstable patients, angry relatives and venturing into unsavory neighborhoods. But her need to help others—provide hope—trumped any threat to her personal safety. She took precautions. She wasn't stupid.

Nick made a noncommittal sound and slowed the vehicle, turning into the parking lot of a nondescript building. A lonely sedan with a dent in the back panel sat in the parking lot. "Good, we caught her."

Her, no doubt, being his sister. The physician.

Sarah's mouth went dry. "I can't. I won't get out of the car."

"My sister's a great doctor. Don't worry."

Sarah glanced around the empty parking lot. The lonely country road beyond that. Her stomach knotted.

Suddenly, she was irrationally angry at this man who, on the surface, only wanted to help her.

"You shouldn't have brought me here," she bit out.

Under the white glow from the spotlights illuminating the building and parking lot, a flash of something raced across his features. For the second time since she had met him earlier tonight, she noticed the vulnerability in his face. He turned to her, a look of apology in his eyes. "Let my sister take a look. Just a look. If after that you want to go home, I'll take you. No questions asked." He cracked his door and the dome light popped on.

Nodding, Sarah squinted against the brightness. Her stomach felt queasy.

The first rule of disappearing—her personal rule—was not to get involved with anyone. Nick

Jennings looked a lot like someone who might be worth breaking a rule for.

If only he weren't a police officer.

Sarah knew more than anyone that sometimes even the guys who were supposed to be good weren't.

Jimmy Braeden, her stalker ex-boyfriend, was a prime example. Her ex was a cop. And if tonight was any indication, he may have finally found her.

Goose bumps raced across her arms and she shuddered. She turned and saw her hollow eyes in the reflection of the passenger window.

"Okay," she said, part agreement, part sigh, "I'll let your sister take a look." Her acquiescence was mostly to get inside, out of the open. Away from the crosshairs of an abusive man who threatened he'd kill her before he'd ever let her go.

TWO

Sarah's vision narrowed tunnellike as she climbed out of the deputy's vehicle in the parking lot of the health-care clinic. In a flash, Nick moved next to her and grabbed her arm. Her first instinct was to pull away.

Run.

She blinked up at him.

"Are you okay? Here, sit." His words sounded distant, jumbled in her ears. She was only partially aware of him yanking open the car door she had just slammed shut and ushering her to a seated position inside his vehicle. He crouched down in front of her and studied her eyes. "Are you dizzy?"

"I stood up too fast." She had learned to make excuses to cover her panic attacks. It was less embarrassing this way. Her feelings were irrational, self-created, yet she couldn't always control them.

"You've had a head injury."

Sarah absentmindedly reached up and touched her head and pulled her fingers away, sticky with her own blood. Her stomach lurched and she shoved back a million memories of another time her head had been bleeding. Back then, the man with her hadn't offered to help. No, it took several hours and a heaping dose of remorse before he came back to her, pleading for forgiveness with a promise to never lift a hand to her again.

Until the next time.

"Do you think you can make it into the clinic? If not, I can get a wheelchair from inside."

Embarrassment edged out her feelings of anxiety, two emotions that twined around her lungs and made it difficult to breathe. "I can walk in." One thing her ex-boyfriend had taught her was to pretend to be tough.

She had gotten good at pretending. At a lot of things.

Sarah stood and the officer hung close by her side, holding her elbow. He obviously wasn't convinced. When they reached the door of the health-care clinic, it was locked. He buzzed the intercom and a crackling voice responded. "Who is it?"

"Christina, it's Nick. I have a patient for you to examine." He was talking into the intercom but his intense brown eyes were locked on hers, unnerving her.

"Urgent?" came his sister's one word response.

"No, a few stitches."

"Not a good idea," Sarah muttered. She tried to pull away, but Nick gripped her arm tighter. She winced and he eased his hold, but not completely. She must have appeared as unsteady as she felt.

"I'm not going to let you go home with a head wound. I don't want to get a call that you ended up dying in your sleep."

Sarah wasn't sure if his words were an exaggeration to wear down her resistance or a flat-out lie. She hardly thought her injury was that serious. "I was cut by glass, not hit by the rock." She lifted her eyebrows and could feel the stiffness of the dried blood on her forehead.

The annoying buzzer released the lock on the door. As the deputy pulled it open, he whispered, "I'm trying to help you. Are you going to fight me every step of the way?"

She shrugged. She imagined she'd thank him one day for insisting she be treated for the cut on her head, sparing her from a lifetime of explaining how she got the scar, but today wasn't that day.

They reached the dated waiting room. Dark

stains—including a now-black piece of bub-
blegum—marred the bluish-gray carpet. Nick
didn't ask her to sit down on one of the blue
plastic chairs, something her pounding head
definitely would have appreciated. Instead he
guided her through the office with a gentle hand
on her waist and found his sister on the phone
in the back.

The attractive woman, her long dark hair
pulled up into a messy bun, mouthed without
making a sound, "Give me a minute." Her gaze
traveled the length of Sarah, a scrutiny Sarah
had tried to avoid at all costs since she had
moved into the small cottage in Apple Creek
and set up her quiet practice through the church.

Sarah's face heated and the urge to flee nearly
overwhelmed her. *Don't have a panic attack.
Don't have a panic attack.*

The physician pointed at the open door of an
adjacent examination room. Nick understood
the silent directive and led Sarah into the room.
At his insistence, she sat on the exam table, the
white, protective paper crinkling as she scooted
back. Nick stood sentinel at her side, and an
awkward silence joined the steady hum of an
air conditioner. Sarah was grateful for the cool
air blowing across her skin.

The doctor's appearance in the doorway was

never more welcomed. Her gaze went from her brother to Sarah and back to her brother.

"Sarah was cut by broken glass. Someone threw a rock through the basement window of the church."

If Sarah hadn't been watching the doctor's face, she might have missed the slight flinch. "The church, huh? Is nothing sacred?"

Sarah lifted a shoulder, finding it difficult to respond.

"I don't have insurance," Sarah repeated her lie. "I can pay over time if that's okay?"

"We treat a lot of patients without insurance. We'll figure something out. First things first." The physician grabbed a clipboard. "Do you mind filling out this form?"

Sarah took the clipboard in her shaky hands and stared at it. Her pulse rushed in her head and the letters forming the words *Name*, *Address*, *Phone number* scrambled in her field of vision. She placed the clipboard down on the crinkly white paper and slid off the table.

Nick gently touched her elbow.

The world shifted around Sarah, and she grabbed the smooth vinyl edge of the table to steady herself. "This was a mistake. I shouldn't have come here."

"You need to have that cut looked at." Nick, in his crisp sheriff's uniform, loomed over her, his commanding voice vibrating through her. The walls grew close. Too close.

Sarah pushed past him. "I don't *have* to do anything."

"Wait," the physician said. Instinctively, Sarah stopped in her tracks. "You." The physician pointed at her brother. "Wait outside." She turned to Sarah. "And you. Please, let me look at your injuries."

A small smile touched the attractive doctor's face. "You don't have to fill out any paperwork."

Sarah let out a long sigh, and without meeting Nick's gaze, she returned to the exam table. The deputy slipped outside and closed the door.

The physician examined her in silence. The young doctor smelled like flowers and coconut lotion. She brushed a damp gauze pad across Sarah's wound. "I'd feel better if we put a few stitches in this cut. I'd hate for you to have a huge scar."

"Do you really think that's necessary, Dr. Jennings?" Sarah didn't notice a wedding ring on her finger, and since she was the deputy's sister, she made the leap that her last name was the same as Nick's.

"Yes, I do. And feel free to call me Christina. If I wanted to be Dr. Jennings I would have stayed at the big research hospital where I did my residency before I opened this clinic."

Christina got out her instruments, and Sarah found herself wrapping her fingers around the edge of the table as another wave of panic crested below the surface.

"Perhaps you should lie down. I'd hate for you to pass out while I'm working on you." With her hand to Sarah's shoulder, Christina guided her patient to a supine position.

Christina cleaned the wound with a cool swab. "I'm glad you caught me. I was about to close up for the night." The doctor ran the back of her protective glove across her forehead. "It's been a long day, and the paperwork is endless."

As Christina leaned in close to examine Sarah's wound, Sarah noticed creases lined the physician's pretty brown eyes, making her a few years older than Sarah first would have guessed.

"Thank you. I appreciate you taking the time. I had tried to tell your brother I didn't need medical attention."

Christina made a sound with her lips pressed together, a cross between an "I see" and "let me make that decision." Sarah didn't ask what she meant by that because she figured it didn't matter. If she got these stitches maybe Nick would leave her alone and she'd resume her quiet life. God willing.

Unless Jimmy had found her...

Sarah swallowed back her nausea, fearing if

she let her worries take root, she'd have a full-blown anxiety attack.

Dear Lord, protect me and please, please, please keep me safe from Jimmy.

They fell into silence as Christina focused on the task of suturing Sarah's wound. After Christina finished, she placed a small bandage across Sarah's forehead near her hairline. Christina smiled at her work. "I think that should heal nicely. My father once suggested I go into plastic surgery, but my heart had more humble goals." Christina's brown eyes met Sarah's as if to say, "So, here I am in this small-town health-care clinic."

Christina held Sarah's hand and helped her swing around to a seated position. The physician tipped her head and met Sarah's eyes. "You feel okay?"

Sarah nodded. *As good as I'm going to feel under the circumstances.* But she kept that thought to herself. She had learned to keep a lot of things to herself over the past six months. And even before that.

Christina turned her back to Sarah and put a few instruments onto a tray. "Is there anything you'd like to share with me?"

Emotion rose in Sarah's throat, and she cut her gaze toward the door. The need for escape was strong. "I don't know what you mean."

Christina turned around slowly. "I've seen a lot working in a rural health-care clinic." She tipped her chin toward the discarded clipboard. "You didn't want to share any personal information. What or *who* are you hiding from?"

Sarah's cheeks flared hot. "I'm…" The lie died on her lips. She had mentally trained herself to deny, deny, deny even though deceit went against her Christian upbringing. White lies were a matter of self-preservation. She prayed God would understand.

Sarah looked at the closed door. Christina was bound by doctor-patient confidentiality. Sarah closed her eyes and made a decision. She'd confide in Christina.

Sarah swallowed around the lump in her throat. "I came to Apple Creek to get away from my ex-boyfriend."

"He's abusive."

"Yes. I feared if I stayed in Buffalo, he'd kill me."

Christina reached out and squeezed Sarah's hand. "I'm sorry." She narrowed her gaze. "Do you think he found you? Do you think he could have been the one to throw the rock through the window? To scare you?"

"No, no. No one knows where I am." Sarah hoped saying the words out loud would make them true.

"No one?"

"Only the pastor and his wife. And our pastor back home. My mother also knows where I am. It gives her some peace to know."

Christina flattened her lips and nodded, as if giving it some thought.

"And my brother?"

Sarah shook her head, her eyes flaring wide. "No, I just met your brother tonight."

"My brother's a deputy. He can protect you."

"My ex-boyfriend's a cop. He's on the force in Orchard Gardens, a suburb of Buffalo." Sarah's voice grew soft, dejected. "He didn't protect me."

Christina twisted her lips. "My brother's a good guy."

Sarah gingerly touched the bandage on her forehead. "A lot of people think Officer Jimmy Braeden is a good guy. Do you know how hard it is to file a police report when his brothers in blue think he's such a great guy?" All the old hurt and pain twisted in her gut. "No thanks."

"I think you'd be safer if someone in law enforcement here in Apple Creek knew to be on the lookout for him. Where do you live?"

A little voice in the back of Sarah's head was growing louder and louder: *Don't tell her. Don't let her in. He'll find you.*

"I rented the cottage on the Zook's property."

A knot in her chest eased a fraction. It felt good to confide in someone. Was Christina right? Should she let Nick in on her secret?

"I don't want anyone else to know what I'm running away from. I'm safer this way," Sarah blurted before she changed her mind.

"What about tonight? Do you think he found you?"

The heat of anxiety rippled across Sarah's skin. "Tonight was just some kids."

"But you don't *know* that."

"There's no way Jimmy knows where I am."

"Are you sure?" The tone of the doctor's voice sent cold shards shooting through Sarah's veins.

Sarah shoved back her shoulders, trying to muster a confidence she didn't feel. "I have stayed off the radar for six months. No car. No credit card purchases. I've been careful about contact with anyone from my past. There's no way he can know I'm here." And if Jimmy had found her, he wouldn't have simply thrown a rock through the window and fled. He would have stayed, stormed into the basement and killed her.

Unless he wanted to terrorize her first. Make a game of it. Jimmy loved nothing more than playing games. Games that were stacked in his favor.

Sarah shook her head both to answer Christina's question and to shake away her constant irrational thoughts. *This* is what Jimmy had done to her. Not just the physical abuse, he had made her question her own sanity.

She had to flee Buffalo to save herself physically, emotionally and professionally. Jimmy was able to poke so many holes in her accusations that her job as a social worker for the county had been in jeopardy.

Christina ran a hand across her chin. "If you're running away, why only go an hour from Buffalo? You could have gone anywhere. The other side of the country."

"It's twofold really. The pastor of my old church had a connection here in Apple Creek. They needed a social worker. And my mother still lives in the area."

"You realize it's dangerous to contact your mother. Your boyfriend—"

"*Ex*-boyfriend."

"Well, he's probably keeping tabs on your mother in case you make contact."

"I haven't. Only through the pastors have we kept in touch. Through letters." Loss and nostalgia clogged her throat. "My mom's sick. I need updates, and I need to be able to run home in an emergency."

Christina bit her lower lip and nodded. Sarah

appreciated that Christina didn't question her need to be near her mom. Just in case.

"If even one person knows where you are, you're in jeopardy," Christina added.

Sarah was about to say something when a quiet knock sounded on the door.

Christina lowered her voice so Nick wouldn't overhear through the door. "If you're not going to leave Apple Creek, I strongly encourage you to confide in my brother. He can protect you," she repeated.

A stark reality weighed heavily on Sarah. If Jimmy Braeden found her, no one could protect her.

"A deputy sheriff's escort to my home is more than enough. You don't have to walk me to the door, *Officer* Jennings." Sarah slowed at the bottom step of her rented cottage and turned to face him, obviously trying her best to put her protective shield back in place. Nick could see it in her eyes. She was refusing his help every step of the way.

What secret was she hiding?

"You were attacked this evening, and whoever did it is still out there."

"I was hardly attacked. Someone threw a rock through a window, and I got in the way. It was probably kids fooling around."

Nick raised an eyebrow. "May I make sure your property's secure?" He framed it as a question, but he wasn't leaving until he made sure she was safe.

"Only in a small town." Sarah shrugged and smiled, an attempt to sound light and breezy, but she wasn't fooling him.

"I'll check the doors and windows."

"Okay." Sarah sounded exhausted.

His cell phone chirped, and he glanced at it and held up his finger.

"Deputy Sheriff Jennings."

"Hey, Nick." It was Lila, the dispatcher. "Sheriff Maxwell caught some kids lurking around behind the general store. They were throwing empty liquor bottles against the wall."

"Any of them confess to shattering the church window?"

"Not yet, but I imagine once we get some of their fathers in here, they'll straighten right quick."

"Amish?"

"Three of the five. Two are townies."

"Are they being held?"

"Yes, at the station. If you want to put the fear of God in them, you should come in quick. I don't imagine they'll be there long."

"Okay." Nick clicked End and looked at Sarah.

"They caught some kids breaking glass bottles behind the general store. No one claims to have thrown a rock through the church window, but it's possible."

An overwhelming need to protect Sarah filled him. What was it about her? Her petite stature? Her vulnerability? Or was he drawn to Sarah's fiery attitude that emerged every time he suggested something she didn't like.

His mind flashed to his sister Christina. She seemed to have her life together now—she lived and breathed the health-care clinic—but there was a time when she, too, had been vulnerable and he hadn't been there to help her. His stomach twisted at the thought of what might have happened if she hadn't gotten away the night she was attacked on campus. His head told him he couldn't be everywhere, but the pain in his heart told him he needed to try. It made him want to be a better officer.

They stood in silence for a minute before Sarah turned and inserted the key into the lock. Most people in Apple Creek didn't lock their doors, but he supposed a single woman living out here all alone wasn't like *most* people.

And enough bad things had happened, even here in Apple Creek, that eventually everyone would realize they're not immune to evil.

Sarah pushed open the door and propped the screen door open with her hip. She turned to face him. "Since they picked up the kids breaking bottles, I'm fine out here." There was a hint of a question in her tone.

"Hold on, you're not slipping away from me that easily."

Sarah narrowed her eyes. He couldn't seem to reach her, and he wasn't sure why he was striking out.

"I'm going to call Sheriff Maxwell and get their names, and you can tell me if you know any of them from your meetings."

Sarah leaned on the doorframe and held the screen door open a fraction with the palm of her hand, apparently still hesitant to allow him into her home.

Once Nick gave the names, Sarah frowned. "Ruben and Ephram Zook live next door." She stretched out her arm and pointed to the well-tended home across the field. "I'm surprised they'd get caught up in such foolishness. I'm renting the house from their parents. Their father is rather strict. However, I suppose saying an Amish father is strict is redundant." The tight set of her mouth relaxed into an all-too-fleeting smile. "But neither boy has been to one of my meetings. I've never heard of them having issues with alcohol or drugs. Or being otherwise wild during *rumspringa*."

"What about the other names?"

Sarah shook her head. "Not familiar to me."

"I'll have to talk to each of them. See if they'd been near the church first."

"Please don't tell anyone you asked if the young Amish men had been to one of my meetings. My work is based on trust. They'll be afraid to come if they think I'll rat them out."

Trust.

Nick nodded. Strange word for a woman who seemed afraid to trust him. She was obviously harboring secrets.

"You going to be okay out here?"

"Yes, I'm fine."

Nick hesitated a fraction before pivoting on his heel and stomping down the porch steps.

Sarah Lynn had secrets. Unless her secrets drew the attention of the Apple Creek sheriff's department, Nick decided he'd let her be.

The last thing he needed was to get caught up with someone like Sarah. It would be easy to do. But Nick had already been burned by a woman with her share of secrets.

Once in a man's lifetime was enough.

Sarah walked through the small cottage she rented—cash only—from the Amish family next door without turning on any lights. The downstairs windows lacked curtains, and she hadn't remedied the situation because she had to be conservative with her money. Make it last. But she hated the lack of privacy. A woman who had a stalker didn't relish the notion of being in a lit-up fish tank. So most nights, she retired to her upstairs bedroom to read in privacy.

How long can I keep hiding? Delaying my life because I'm afraid of one man?

Sarah reached the kitchen. The white moonlight slanted across the neat and functional cabinets and stove. *Englischers*, as the Amish called people like her, had lived here and when they moved away, Amos Zook had purchased the house adjacent to his land for future use by one of his children. Therefore, the house had modern amenities, such as they were, that would have to be torn out once one of the sons and his new bride moved into the house. Perhaps when Ruben, their second-eldest son, married Mary Ruth. If the rumor mill was to be believed. When Sarah first heard the plans for the house, she found it amusing. Updating a home by removing modern conveniences.

Sarah opened a cabinet closest to the sink and got a glass for water. As the cool liquid slid down her throat, her mind drifted to her mother. Alone in the only home Sarah had ever known.

She and her mother had been exchanging letters through their pastors. Her mother's were always filled with cheery accounts of what she had been up to depending on the day and the weather.

"Weeded the garden today. You should see your father's rosebushes." Her father had been dead twenty years, but his rosebushes kept thriving.

"Wow, had to shovel the walkway three times today. I don't think spring is ever going to get here."

Or…

"It's been so hot that I've had to turn on the fan at night. You know how I hate to sleep with that fan."

Despite her mother's lung cancer diagnosis almost a year ago, Sarah rarely ever heard her mother complain about her health. And when it came time to flee Buffalo because of Jimmy, her mother encouraged her to go and live her life, happy and healthy and away from that domineering man.

Her mother made it sound like her last wish: that her daughter live a happy life. Perhaps the kind of life that had eluded her mother after she lost her husband in a drunk-driving accident.

Pinpricks of tears bit at the back of her eyes. Losing a dad as a little kid did that to a person. Her poor dad had gone out for ice cream when some drunk teenager T-boned him at an intersection. Sarah inhaled through her nose and exhaled through her mouth, a trick she had learned to calm her anxiety. It worked maybe half the time.

Sarah glanced around the dark kitchen, and her cheeks flushed. Her mother had been widowed when Sarah was only ten. She raised Sarah to be a confident, independent woman. It shamed Sarah that she had fallen for a man who was able to control her.

Instead of following her mother's lead, Sarah had grown up fearful, cautious, contained.

Now she'd have to spend the rest of her days hiding. And pray she'd get to visit her mother again in person before the horrible disease took its toll.

A rush of nostalgia overwhelmed her, and the sudden urge to call her mother nearly brought her to tears. Sarah moved to the kitchen hutch in the darkness and opened the middle drawer. It opened with a creak, sending shivers up and down her spine. Sarah hated that she had grown fearful of her own shadow. Yet, she had turned Nick away when he volunteered to check her house. Such was the conundrum of being stalked by a cop.

Afraid, but too afraid to call the police.

Glancing around the darkened space of her current home, she convinced herself she was alone. Safe, but alone. She laughed, an awkward sound in the silence.

Boy, am I ever alone.

Leaning down, she stretched her arm to the back of the drawer. There, she found the disposable phone and a prepaid card with one hundred minutes. Items she had purchased—*with cash*—in a moment of weakness, but then never used. Sometimes just knowing she had a phone, a way to reach out, made her feel less lonely.

Tonight she had reached her breaking point. No one could trace the call, she reasoned. She needed her mom. What girl didn't? She needed to hear her mother's reassuring voice. Tonight of all nights.

Sarah flipped on a light. Her hands shook with the knowledge of what she was about to do. Sarah fumbled with the packaging until she freed the phone. It fell and clattered against the pine table in her kitchen. She scooped it up and held it close to her beating heart, feeling as if she were doing something criminal.

The tiny hairs on her arms stood on edge and she couldn't shake that feeling that someone was watching her. She lifted her head and stared toward the back window, her reflection caught in the glass. Beyond that, the yard was pitch-black. A surge of icy dread coursed through her veins. She'd have to save up for curtains. Sitting here like a duck on a target stand with a big red bull's-eye over her head didn't do anything for her nerves.

She gathered up the phone's instructions and turned off the lamp. She hurried into the downstairs bathroom, closed the door and turned on the light to read the instructions. In short order—after installing the battery and activating the phone—she was calling the familiar phone number of her childhood home. The same phone number Sarah had since the time she could reach her mother's rotary phone mounted on the wall in the kitchen. The phone had been updated, but little else had in her mother's cozy home.

Yeah, the Gardners didn't have the fanciest gadgets, but they did have each other. Sort of.

With shaky fingers, Sarah pressed the last digit of her home phone number and held her breath. Silence stretched across the phone for a long time. Sarah pulled it away from her ear and glanced at it, wondering if it actually worked. A distant ringing sounded in the quiet space, and Sarah quickly pressed the phone to her ear. It was getting late, but she knew her mother didn't sleep much nowadays.

...Three, four, five...

She counted the rings.

"Come on, Mom, answer the phone."

She imagined her mother pushing off the recliner—maybe asleep in front of whatever show happened to be on right now—muttering about the nerve of someone calling so late. No matter how many times she told her mother to keep the portable phone by her side, her mother insisted on placing it in the charger.

Every. Time.

...*Eight, nine...*

Sarah's body hummed with impatience.

"Hello," came her mother's curt greeting, startling Sarah who had all but given up hope that she'd reach her mom tonight.

Sarah swallowed a knot of emotion. "Mom." The word came out high-pitched and tight.

"Sarah..." her mother said her name on a hopeful sigh.

"Yeah, it's me."

Her mother's tone shifted from surprised delight to concern. "Is everything okay?"

Sarah touched the bandage on her head. "Yeah, yeah, I just missed you and needed to hear your voice."

Her mother made an indecipherable sound and started to cough, a wet, popping noise. Her mother tried to talk, but the racking cough consumed her.

Sadness, helplessness and terror seized Sarah's heart.

She envisioned her mother reaching for a tissue and holding it in a tight fist against her mouth as her pale face grew red from the exertion of coughing. Her eyes watering. A loud gasp sounded across the line as her mom struggled to catch her breath.

Sarah muttered a curse against Jimmy. She should be there caring for her mother. Not hiding an hour away, alone in someone else's house.

After a moment, when the coughing slowed, Sarah asked, "Are you okay?"

Her mother seemed to have collected herself. "I think I'm coming down with a cold."

Her poor, sweet mother, always trying to protect her only daughter. Sarah hadn't magically forgotten that her mother had lung cancer.

"Have you been keeping up with your doctor's appointments?"

"Yes. There's just so many. Sometimes I'll have a coughing jag when I'm driving…" Her mother forced a cheery tone. "Now, don't worry about me. I'm as tough as they come. Now tell me about you. I thought we were only supposed to write letters. Safer that way."

"I called on a disposable phone."

Silence stretched across the line. "Jimmy came here the other day."

Sarah's heart jackhammered in her chest. "What did he want?" *You, stupid, stupid girl!*

Suddenly the phone felt like a hot coal in her hand. What if he tracked her down here? How? It was a disposable phone.

Jimmy was resourceful.

She looked up at the lavender walls of the small downstairs half bath. She'd have to run again. This time farther away. Away from her mother.

"Jimmy acted like he was checking up on me, seeing if I needed anything—boy, that man could charm a lollipop from a baby—but I knew better. He was fishing around to see if I knew where you were. Same as he's done the other times he's swung by the house on the guise of checking up on me."

Sarah pressed the phone tighter to her ear, her racing pulse making it more difficult to hear. "What did you tell him?" Sarah's mouth grew dry as she anticipated her mother's answer. They had rehearsed before Sarah left as to what her mother should say or do, but Sarah constantly worried that her mother's illness, medication or just a plain old slip of the tongue would jeopardize her location.

Sarah knew she was being irrational, but having someone mess with your mind for two years straight had forced an otherwise sane girl to consider every crazy scenario.

Her mother started coughing again, but regained her composure more quickly this time. "I told him what we agreed upon. *Again*. That you had a job opportunity in California. Lord, forgive me for lying, but I do it to keep you safe."

"I imagine he's pressing you for an address. A phone number."

"I told him it was best if he moved on now."

Sarah could imagine Jimmy's reaction when he was told to give up on something. Jimmy Braeden wasn't a quitter. Or one who liked to lose. And losing Sarah had come as a huge blow to his ego.

"Mom, there's no way Jimmy believes I moved to California for a job. Not when you're not feeling well." *Not feeling well.* That was an understatement. "He's going to keep pushing." Maybe they should have come up with a different story.

Jimmy would never stop looking for her. That much she knew for sure. Knees feeling weak, Sarah grabbed the towel bar and lowered herself onto the closed toilet lid. She reached forward and turned the lock on the bathroom door.

One swift nudge with a strong shoulder would send the door into splinters. How pitiful. She had locked herself into the bathroom of the home where she lived alone.

"I'm sorry I'm not there for you." Sarah fought to keep the tears from her voice.

"I'm managing fine."

Sarah cleared her throat. "What did the doctor say last time you were there?"

She envisioned her mom waving her hand in dismissal. "Oh, the same as always. If I believed everything they told me, I'd be buried next to your father already."

Cold dread pooled in Sarah's stomach. She feared her mother would never tell her the truth when it came to her prognosis.

Sarah traced the round edge of the brass door handle. "Maybe it's time I came home."

"I'm fine." Her mother's forced cheeriness sounded shrill. They both knew Sarah returning to Buffalo would only add more stress to her mother's already stressed life. And they both knew Jimmy was a violent man who had the backing of his brothers in uniform—both in Orchard Gardens where he worked and his fellow cops in nearby Buffalo. All the cops seemed to know each other. Yet, Sarah couldn't fault the men. Jimmy was a great liar and friend, when he wasn't beating up his girlfriend. She didn't blame his fellow cops for being deceived. Hadn't she been? When Sarah tried to make a report, Jimmy's own mother gave him an alibi. Then the rumors began when Sarah showed up at the station with a black eye.

Sarah had been out drinking and picked up

the wrong guy. Now to save face, she's trying to blame it on Officer Braeden because they just went through a bad breakup.

It was then that she knew she'd never get justice. And if she valued her life and her mother's peace of mind, she had to leave.

Sarah pulled off a strip of toilet paper and wiped her nose. "Maybe you and I can go off somewhere. Somewhere where Jimmy can't find us."

"Sarah…Sarah…" her mother said, in her familiar soothing voice that made Sarah's chest ache with nostalgia. "We've been through all this. I need to stay close to my doctors. And I like my home. Tending the garden." *I want to be in my own bed when I die.* Her mother didn't say it, but it was implied.

Sarah swallowed around the knot of emotion in her throat.

"Have you made any friends where you are? Someone you can trust?"

Nick's kind smile floated to mind. "It's hard, Mom. I don't know who I can trust." However, Sarah *had* confided in Nick's sister, but Christina was bound by doctor-patient confidentiality. And sweet, Amish Mary Ruth would never understand her new friend's predicament.

And Sarah didn't trust her own decision-making skills. She had been wrong—so very wrong—before.

"You need to stay safe," her mom said, her voice cracking. "*Please*, I love you."

"I love you, too, Mom. I'll stay here."

"That's my girl. Go and save the world." Her mother liked to tout that her only daughter was always looking for ways to help people. Too bad Sarah didn't know how to help herself.

THREE

The next morning, Nick grabbed two large coffees—one black, one double cream, double sugar—and headed to his sister's clinic. When he arrived, the first rays of sun were poking over the full foliage of the trees. He could already tell it was going to be a scorcher today. They were in the dog days of summer, and in a few short months, everyone would be grumbling about the snow and cold.

He glanced at the clock on his dash. The clinic didn't open for another thirty minutes, but he knew his sister would already be doing paperwork and preparing for the day. Both he and his sister were workaholics in jobs that served the public. Nick always figured that had a lot to do with their upbringing, the children of two entrepreneurs who made and lost their first fortune before they were thirty-five and made it again by forty. The second time was a keeper.

All the children could have gone into the family business—only their younger sister Kelly had—and continued to live a life of privilege, but instead Christina and Nick seemed determined to save the world. Their parents, although wealthy and living lives unimaginable by most, had been philanthropists and had made things like Christina's health-care clinic possible. Linda and John Jennings were well respected in Apple Creek even though they only touched down at their home base once or twice a year.

Nick went around back to the alley and found his sister's car parked next to the back door. He tried the handle, but found it locked. He was relieved. Christina was a smart, compassionate doctor and street savvy. Even in small towns, addicts and other low-life criminals sought out drugs from whatever source they could find them. He was glad his sister took her safety seriously.

Juggling the stacked coffees in one hand, he pulled out his cell phone and texted Christina.

At back door

A few seconds later the door opened. Christina initially looked like she was going to scold him for bothering her this early, but when her eyes landed on the coffee, a bright smile crossed her features.

Christina was his little sister, younger by three years. The two of them grew up in Apple Creek and mostly only had each other and Kelly as playmates on their parents' sprawling estate. Their mom and dad, both self-employed, could work from anywhere, and when Nick, Christina and Kelly were young, they decided the tranquility of Apple Creek was as good a place as any to build a home.

"Double cream, double sugar?" Christina reached out with the look of a woman in need of a caffeine fix.

"Of course. First coffee of the day?"

"Yes, I usually wait until the office staff comes in to start the coffeemaker."

Christina stepped back, allowing her brother entry into the clinic. She peeled back the brown lid from the takeout coffee and inhaled the scent.

"You really love that stuff."

Christina laughed. "Love is a strong word." She took a long sip with her eyes closed, then lifted them to study him. "What brings you here bright and early, big brother?" She held up her hand. "Oh, let me guess. Does it have anything to do with a pretty, petite blonde who got three stitches in her forehead last night?"

"Am I that transparent?" A corner of his mouth quirked up.

"I'm your sister. You've always worn your heart on your sleeve."

"This has nothing to do with my heart."

Christina arched a skeptical brow. "Really?" She put the coffee down and sat on the corner of her desk and crossed her arms over her chest.

"I know you can't break doctor-patient confidentiality."

"But you're hoping I might?"

"No, but is there something I need to know? To protect her."

Christina laughed. "Right. You're looking for an excuse to talk to her again. I don't blame you. It's been, what…a year or so since you and Amber went your separate ways."

Just the mention of the name Amber sent Nick's mood spiraling into the depths of the foulest garbage dump. He and Amber had met five years ago at a Christmas party at his parents' home. They hit it off and had been inseparable until Nick was deployed. Turned out, Amber wasn't the kind to wait. Turned out, Amber and someone—Troy or Trey or something like that—were secretly dating behind his back.

Amber sent him a Dear John letter while he was still deployed. It was like getting punched while dodging IEDs.

"Yeah, do me a favor, don't mention Amber."

Nick hadn't dated anyone seriously since. He didn't trust his instincts. He had thought Amber was the one. Turns out so did Troy/Trey. They were married a few months ago at the country club. Their wedding had been featured prominently on the front page of the LifeStyle section of the newspaper. Nick suspected Amber loved money more than him, and when she realized he wasn't going to follow in his parents' footsteps, she decided she had better find another meal ticket.

The coffee roiled in his gut. *How had he not seen through Amber?*

Christina pushed off her desk and turned around to fumble with some neatly stacked papers. He knew his sister well enough to know she was struggling to decide how much to tell him about Sarah.

Nick respected her job, the need for confidentiality. But he'd also hate to ignore his instincts on this one. Sure, his dating instincts were terrible, but his law enforcement instincts were usually spot-on.

Sarah was afraid of something. More than a rock thrown through the basement window.

Christina picked up a clipboard and held it close to her chest. "You might want to pay Sarah a visit. You could tell her you're following up from last night. I think she needs someone to talk to."

He studied his sister closely.

"And hey, maybe you could ask her out for dinner."

Nick's head jerked back. "I'm done with women with secrets."

Christina pinned him with her gaze. "You're going to have to get over Amber."

"I'm over her."

Christina didn't say anything, suggesting she doubted him. "Then, go out and visit Sarah. Maybe you'll surprise yourself."

"I don't make a habit of asking crime victims out on a date."

Christina touched his arm. "Will you please get over yourself? We live in a small town. If an attractive young woman happens to move here, there's nothing wrong with asking her out on a date."

Nick felt flustered in only the way a little sister could fluster a big brother. "I didn't come out here to ask you for dating advice. I came as a sheriff's deputy to ask you if there's something I should know about our newest resident."

Christina frowned. "And you know full well I couldn't tell you." With both her hands planted on his chest, she shoved him playfully toward the door. He put one hand on the lid of his coffee to prevent it from spilling.

Nick stepped out onto the pavement of the back alley, the sun now above the trees. Christina held the door open with her shoulder. She tapped the metal trim on the bottom of the door with her black loafers. "Sarah could use a friend."

Nick studied his sister's face. Christina was the only one who truly got him. He smiled. "Go finish your coffee before it gets cold."

A shrill buzz sounded from inside the clinic. Someone was at the front door. "Looks like duty calls."

"Have a good day, little sis."

"You, too. Be safe."

Nick waved and watched as the door slammed shut. Instinctively he tested the lock, making sure his sister was secure in the clinic. He knew he couldn't protect everyone at all times…but he'd sure try.

The image of Sarah's pretty face filled his mind. His gut told him she was in need of protecting.

Sarah flipped back the covers on her purple-and-pink bedspread with oversize tulips and gazed around her childhood bedroom. She glanced down at her favorite Holly Hob-

bie nightgown and ran her hand along its soft fabric. Even in her dream, Sarah knew she was dreaming. *She turned her gaze to the corner. Her dolly was tucked under a quilt her mother had made in a crib her father had taken special pride in crafting.*

Sarah had had a charmed childhood. Until that fateful day...

Sarah's dreaming self flipped her legs over the edge of the bed and swung them, trying to take it all in. Trying to memorize every detail of this dream. Hoping her father would come in to kiss her goodnight. To say their evening prayers together.

Feelings of warmth and nostalgia made her smile.

Sarah stretched her legs and curled her toes into the shag rug shaped in the form of a rainbow. She loved that rug. She had spent countless hours with her dollies on that rug pretending they lived in a retro 70s apartment.

Bang! Bang!

Still dreaming, Sarah snapped her attention to the closed bedroom door.

Thud...thud...thud.

Sarah rolled over, consciousness seeping into her dream world. She cracked her eyes open a slit, and a stream of sunshine slipped in through the edge of the white roller shades. Her Amish-made quilt was pretty, but not the same as her childhood favorite. The quilt had slid off the edge of her bed during her fitful dreams. She blinked a few times, trying to recall the last one. The warm fuzziness of it. The return to her childhood.

She smiled and stretched. Talking to her mom last night had made for some vivid dreams. She was surprised she had even slept. She had tossed and turned for hours, until finally getting up around four in the morning. She had gone downstairs, got a glass of water and written in her journal a bit. Her journal kept her sanity, allowing her to empty her mind of her worst fears and worries. Allowing her mind to quiet so she could drift off to sleep.

Sighing, Sarah swung her legs over the edge of the bed. Her toes touched the smooth wood of the pine floor. Nothing to curl her toes into. Maybe she'd buy herself an area rug. Undoubtedly the Apple Creek General Store probably didn't carry what she was looking for. The market for 70s shag here in Apple Creek was slim to nonexistent.

A distant thought niggled at her brain. Had something woken her up? A sound? Sarah rolled her shoulders. She was probably still spooked from the incident last night at the church. Lifting her hand, she touched the bandage on her forehead and groaned.

She'd get lots of questions today from her clients. She'd mention the broken window, but play it off. She preferred to keep the focus on them. Not her.

Sarah quickly got ready for the day and twirled her hair into a ponytail. Living out here in the country, she had come to enjoy jeans, a T-shirt, no makeup and no-fuss hair. In many ways it was freeing.

Jimmy preferred it when she was all made up.

Sarah jogged down the stairs and froze with her hand on the railing. The front door stood ajar. She took a step back and lost her balance, landing on her backside on the stairs. She pulled herself up by the railing. Her heart beat wildly in her ears. She bent and leaned over the railing, trying to see if someone had come into her house. She hadn't left the door open last night.

Or unlocked.

And her house was secure when she had gotten up in the middle of the night.

She bit her lower lip, and her legs went to Jell-O.

Had Jimmy found her after all? Picked the lock? Had it been a coincidence that some boys had been caught smashing bottles against an alley wall near the church where a window was broken?

Cautiously, she descended the remaining stairs, listening for any out-of-place creak, voice, breath…anything that would indicate she wasn't alone. She inhaled deeply through her nose, wondering if she could detect Jimmy's cologne, a scent that often lingered in a room long after he had left.

Nothing.

Leaving the door open—it would serve as a quick escape if she needed it—Sarah tiptoed through the sitting room and into the kitchen. She stiffened in the doorway, panic sending ripples of goose bumps racing across her flesh.

Her hand flew to her mouth to cover a silent scream. There on the table were the remains of a thick snake, its head cut off and placed on top of the phone she had used last night. The phone she had carefully tucked back into the center drawer of the hutch. Her diary sat on the edge of the table where she had left it.

Nerves on edge, she backed up.

Get out! Get out!

A solid chest and firm hands on her arms stopped her backward progression.

A scream ripped from her throat.

FOUR

"It's okay. It's me." Nick released his grasp on Sarah's arms and stepped around in front of her so she could see him. "It's Nick Jennings. You're okay."

Sarah clamped her mouth shut and a hint of embarrassment touched the corners of her eyes.

Nick's gaze drifted from her frightened face to the tableau on Sarah's kitchen table. "What happened here?" He quickly glanced around the room.

"Do you think I honestly know?" Her voice held more than an edge of annoyance. "I came downstairs and found this." She jabbed her index finger at the coiled-up snake on her kitchen table. She picked up a small book on the edge of the table and slipped it into the hutch.

"Was your front door open when you came downstairs?" He made the logical leap, having found the door yawning open upon his arrival.

"Yes." She rubbed her forehead and winced

when she made contact with the bandage. "I don't understand. I locked up last night after you left."

"You didn't hear anything?"

Sarah shook her head; all the color had drained from her already pale face.

"I came down around four in the morning to get a glass of water. There was nothing on the table then—I'm sure of it. I mean, other than my notebook." With a shaky hand, she pointed toward the hutch where she had just put the book. "Whoever did this, did it in the early-morning hours."

Nick tipped his head, looking out the back kitchen window. From here, he could see a couple Amish boys doing chores at the neighboring barn. "Maybe someone next door saw something. I'll go pay them a visit."

"Ephram and Ruben Zook were picked up last night for smashing bottles, remember? I don't think they're going to want to talk to you." Sarah pulled out a chair and sat down heavily. She moved as if to put her elbows on the table when she grimaced at the proximity of the snake and slumped against the tall wooden back of the chair and crossed her arms. Every muscle in her body seemed to be trembling.

"Did they admit to throwing the rock through

the church window?" Sarah looked up at Nick with a hint of hope in her eyes that he didn't understand.

"No. Only a few bottles were smashed. They hadn't meant any harm and promised to clean it up today. Apparently, they were returning home after the Sunday singings when they ran into some of their *Englisch* friends." He lifted his palms. "Might have been a case of hanging out with the wrong crowd."

Sarah rubbed the back of her neck. "Let's leave them out of this then. I don't want to stir up any more trouble."

"That ship has sailed. Between last night and this morning, it seems you have poked a hornet's nest."

She looked up at him with an unreadable expression.

He leaned in closer to examine a cell phone under a severed snake's head. *Gruesome.* He frowned. "I have a hard time believing the same person who threw a rock through the window did this." He winced at the putrid smell. "Dismembering animals? That's sick." He shook his head. "Not to mention breaking and entering."

Sarah rubbed the back of her neck but didn't say anything.

"Is there anything else you might want to share with me?" Nick thought of the vague reference his sister had made. Did Sarah have dark secrets that put her in jeopardy? Or had some punks thought it would be great fun to harass a single woman living out in the country on her own?

Sarah's weary gaze shifted to the badge on his uniform, then up to his face. The brief moment of vulnerability disappeared and was replaced by an inscrutable expression. "No. I don't know who did this."

"What are you hiding?" Nick's job always had him pushing for the truth from people who often weren't willing to offer it.

Was she a fugitive?

The unlikely scenario flitted from his brain when footsteps sounded on the front porch. "Hello," called a woman with the lilt he recognized as belonging to the Amish.

Nick moved to the front door. Sarah followed close behind.

Nick stepped into the doorway and was greeted by an Amish woman with a young Amish girl by her side. Sarah slipped next to him and paused in the doorway. Standing this close to her emphasized how petite and vulnerable she was.

"Good morning, Temperance," Sarah greeted the Amish woman, then her gaze dropped to the little girl, no more than seven or eight years old, holding her mother's hand. "Morning, Patience."

Temperance fidgeted with the apron on her dress. "Is everything okay? We noticed you had law enforcement over here. I know my boys got in some trouble last night. This doesn't have anything to do with that, does it? They said they weren't near the church." The Amish woman's gaze drifted from Nick to the bandage on her neighbor's head. "My boys are *gut*. They wouldn't have damaged a church."

Sarah lifted her hand and touched the bandage gingerly. "I know. Ruben and Ephram have been nothing but helpful to me."

"Is everything okay this morning?" Temperance asked.

Sarah waved her hand in dismissal. "I'm fine. Deputy Jennings was checking up on me." Nick had never actually told her why he had shown up this morning. Checking in on her was part of it. The other was to see if she was in any real danger. Based on the circumstances, he'd have to go with yes.

As if reading his mind, Sarah squared her shoulders and stepped onto the porch. Was she trying to block the view into her home to make sure her neighbor's young daughter wasn't frightened by the dead snake on the table? Nick doubted they'd be able to see all the way into the kitchen. To be sure, Nick joined her and pulled the door closed behind him. "Hate to let bugs into the house."

"Everything's okay." Sarah smiled at the child. "You want to come over later and we'll read more of Laura Ingalls Wilder?"

The little girl smiled brightly, but her mother took her by the shoulders and guided her toward the porch steps. "Patience has a few chores to do. I don't know if she'll have time for stories."

Sarah's shoulders sagged, and the small smile slid from her lips. "Okay." The single word held so much disappointment.

Temperance brushed at an imaginary spot on her cape. "We wanted to make sure everything was *gut* over here. That's all. We have a lot to do on the farm."

The two guests said their goodbyes, and Sarah's eyes followed the pair as they crossed the yard to their home next door.

"Temperance is usually friendlier to me," Sarah said, almost as if musing to herself. "She must be upset that I got her boys into trouble."

"You didn't get her boys into trouble. They made their own decision when they smashed the bottles. Besides, the Amish aren't partial to law enforcement. Maybe once they knew you were okay, they were eager to leave because of me." Nick wanted to run the back of his fingers across the porcelain skin of her cheek and give her the "it's not you, it's me" speech, but he knew better. She was a stranger, really. Prior to last night, he had only passed her with little more than a "Hello" or "Goodbye" in small-town Apple Creek.

Sarah sat down on the top step of the porch. Her pink toes curved around the edge of the step. "What brought you out here this morning, *Deputy* Jennings?" She emphasized his title, as if it were a bad thing. "Did your sister talk to you?"

Walking over to the railing, he rubbed the back of his neck. He leaned back against the railing so that they were almost back-to-back. He turned to study her serious profile. It was as if she didn't want to make eye contact. "It's not what you think. My sister always respects doctor-patient confidentiality."

"But you suspected something more was going on than a rock through a church window?"

Nick let the silence stretch between them. A gust of wind rustled up and bent the corn stalks growing in the fields next to her house.

Sarah ran a hand down her long ponytail and shifted to face him, a serious expression in her bright blue eyes. "I'm afraid he's found me."

Her shoulders drew up, then came down on a heavy sigh.

Nick jerked his head back, and he pushed off the railing. He slipped past her on the steps and turned around to face her so he could look into her eyes. "Who found you?" Nick didn't understand the protective urge he felt for this woman. He hardly knew her.

Sarah gave him a cynical look and no longer seemed to want to talk to him.

"You know the person who broke into your house? Do you think he also threw the rock last night?"

He studied her. Her blond bangs framed her face, hiding most of the bandage covering her stitches. "I'm afraid I do."

Frustration grew in his belly. "Stop being coy and start talking if you want me to help you."

"I didn't ask for your help." She stared at him, anger flashing in her eyes, before she looked away.

"My job is to help you." Then he softened his tone. "Who has an ax to grind with you?"

"I'm a social worker. I'm sure I have lots of enemies." Was she suddenly backpedalling?

Nick tilted his head and tried to coax her to look at him, but she seemed more focused on the street behind him. "You said you thought you knew who did this."

Sarah bowed her head and threaded her fingers behind her neck. "My ex-boyfriend found me. Now he's going to toy with me until I go running back home. Where he can protect me." Cynicism and defeat laced her tone. "It's the only explanation." She narrowed her gaze but still didn't look at him. "He must really think I'm stupid."

"You ran away from your ex-boyfriend?" Hot blood pumped through his veins.

Her head snapped up, and she directed her fiery gaze at him. "It's not like I had a choice."

"I didn't..." Nick forced his hands to relax, and he sat down on the step next to her. "I'm sorry, I didn't mean to sound accusatory. I have zero tolerance for men who hit women..."

"That makes two of us." She laughed, a brittle sound. "I put up with him for longer than I should have." She shook her head slowly. "I couldn't believe I had turned into one of those women who lets men—" she seemed to be struggling for the right word "—control them. My mother raised me better." The summer sunlight shimmered in unshed tears. He resisted the urge to pull her into an embrace.

"You did nothing wrong," he said, trying to comfort her with his words, all he had a right to offer.

"I didn't have a choice."

"What about the police?"

"He is the police." Sarah studied him as he absorbed that piece of information.

"Where?"

"In a small town right outside of Buffalo. Orchard Gardens." She sounded resigned, sad. "I lived in Buffalo, but he knew a lot of guys on the force there, too. I didn't know who to trust."

"Why didn't you tell me this last night?"

Her gaze locked on the badge on his chest. Then she lifted her wounded eyes to meet his.

"Do you think we belong to one big fraternity? That we'll protect each other no matter what?"

"That's what happened at home. Jimmy can be persuasive. He concocted some story that was so convincing that the other officers thought I was crazy. That I had a drinking problem and was using him to cover it up."

"I'm sorry."

He caught her hiking a skeptical eyebrow.

"You can trust me." The words sounded strange on his lips. Here he was telling her she could trust him, when he had his own trust issues.

"I don't know who to trust anymore. So few people know where I am, I don't know how he found me."

"We don't know that for sure."

"It seems like the only logical answer."

He watched myriad emotions play across her face. He wished he knew her—the situation—well enough to offer her solid advice. Instead he asked, "What do you plan to do now?"

"I don't know." She ran a finger along the tender skin under her eye. "I guess I'll have to move. Again."

Six months.

Six. Short. Months. Apparently that's the expiration date on keeping secrets. It took six months for Officer Jimmy Braeden to find Sarah. Now she'd have to move. Again.

But for now, she had to sit. Focus. Figure out her next step.

Life seemed surreal sitting on her front porch next to Deputy Jennings. She had a hard time thinking of him as simply Nick. He really seemed to care about her well-being, but was his interest genuine?

What if he knows Jimmy? Buffalo isn't that far away, and law enforcement is one big boys' club. Dread pooled in her stomach. *Has Jimmy asked him to keep tabs on me? Or am I being overly dramatic?* Seeing a dead snake sliced up on her table could do that to a girl living alone.

Or maybe this was how small-town cops operated. Making personal visits to the victim the next morning. No nefarious intent.

Sarah blinked and refocused her eyes on the stalks of corn swaying in the morning breeze in the field across the street. There was a sense of timelessness about sitting out here on the farmhouse steps, where a farmer and his family once lived over a hundred years ago.

"Maybe the Amish are on to something?" Sarah's gaze drifted to the farm next door.

"What's that?" Nick's smooth, deep voice had a soothing quality. He turned and they locked gazes. Half his mouth crooked into a wry grin. If she was being truthful, she'd admit to herself how handsome he was. Longish wavy dark hair swept off his face and behind his ears, the ends brushing against his collar. A neatly trimmed goatee on his chin.

A breeze picked up, and a hint of aloe and soap mingled with the corn and freshly chopped hay. She quickly dismissed her keen sense of awareness of him. She had been alone too long. She refocused her attention on the farm next door. Her Amish neighbors made their life off the land, dependent on no one, save for the small rent she paid on this house.

"The Amish live a quiet life. Each generation following in the steps of the one before them. Very little changing." She thought of Mary Ruth, her young Amish friend, who liked to chat about her future. She seemed so full of hope. Sarah didn't know what hope felt like anymore. Didn't know if she'd ever have hope again. Would she forever have to hide from Jimmy?

Sarah ran a hand down her bare arm. The heat from the sun was already strong, beating down on her. If she sat here much longer, she'd be sunburned. She laughed to herself. That was the least of her worries.

She reached up and grabbed the railing and pulled herself to her feet. She swiped the dust of the porch from the back of her pants.

"I have a meeting with a client later today."

"An Amish client?"

"Not today." But it wasn't unusual to see Amish clients. Not all was right within the Amish world. The young adults seemed to struggle the most as the temptations of the outside world crept into their insular lifestyle, tainting it. "It's with a single mom. I can't cancel the meeting. Not at the last minute."

Sarah decided she'd explain to her client that a personal matter had come up and she wouldn't be able to make future meetings. A tiny piece of her heart broke. How long would it be before another social worker took her place? She sighed. Maybe never. "I'll have to come up with a plan for my next move."

Nick stood and faced her. "Do you think that's a good idea?"

"Deputy Jennings—"

"Call me Nick," he said again. She was trying to avoid calling him by his given name, believing the formality would keep a wall between them.

"As long as we're talking names, my full name is Sarah Lynn Gardner. I've used Sarah Lynn to protect my identity. But I suppose that's not relevant anymore."

Sarah gazed at him warily. "I left my sick mother in Buffalo to hide here in Apple Creek. Apparently, I wasn't adept at staying under the radar." She shrugged. "Maybe my next move should be home. Since Jimmy's going to find me anyway…" The sound of her mother's breathless gasps over the phone broke her heart. "I'm afraid my mother won't be around much longer."

"I'm sorry about your mother."

"Me, too." She paused with her hand on the doorknob. "I'm beginning to think that no matter what I do, it won't be the right thing. I have to be able to live with myself. And right now, I'm thinking I'll live with regret for the rest of my life if my mother dies when I'm not there."

"How would your mother feel if your ex-boyfriend killed you?"

Sarah spun around, anger pumping through her veins. "Low blow."

"Your ex must be violent if you're hiding here."

She nodded, a lump clogging her throat. Jimmy was capable of doing almost anything. She had promised her mother she'd stay safe. Running back to Jimmy's home turf wasn't staying safe. Putting herself in jeopardy would be going against her mother's wishes.

And wouldn't she be putting her mother in jeopardy, too?

And how could Sarah abandon her clients here? It was unlikely another social worker would move to Apple Creek anytime soon. Sarah pressed her fingers to her temple, a headache forming behind her eyes.

"Are you okay?" Nick asked, his voice low and full of concern. "I didn't mean to be so blunt." If she hadn't sworn off all men, he'd be someone she'd be drawn to. Too bad she wasn't interested in starting a relationship. And especially not with another cop.

"I'm getting a headache."

"You said earlier that social workers are often the target of disgruntled clients."

"Yeah…" she replied, wondering what he was getting at.

"Before you uproot your entire life here in

Apple Creek, let me do some investigating. Maybe those boys caught throwing bottles in town last night really do know something about this." Nick pointed at her front door, indicating the dismembered snake inside.

Sarah rubbed her arms. A flicker of hope blossomed in her belly. Some angry Amish boys seemed a whole lot less threatening than six-foot-four Jimmy Braeden. However, the dismembered snake head placed on her phone— the one she had used for the first time to call her mom—sent renewed dread pulsing through her heart.

It had to be Jimmy.

It had to be.

"I'm going to talk to Ephram and Ruben Zook. They were part of the group last night." Nick slowed at the bottom of the porch steps.

Sarah paused with her hand on the doorknob. Closing her eyes briefly, her shoulders sagged. "They're good boys. Perhaps just caught up with the wrong kids last night."

"Maybe they can shed some light on what happened."

"Like I said before, they're not going to want to talk to you."

"I'll play nice."

"Temperance's sons don't strike me as the

kind to get into trouble. Ruben has been courting Mary Ruth Beiler, one of the Amish girls who I've grown fond of." Sarah scratched her head.

"It's not unusual for the Amish to blow off some steam after the Sunday-night singings. They *are* teenagers after all." Sarah touched her bandage and winced. "Maybe it's not such a good idea for you to go over there. I don't want to cause any trouble. Amos, their father, has been kind enough to rent me this house. Temperance brings me vegetables from their garden. I don't want to stir up trouble for them."

Climbing the steps to close the distance between them, Nick held up his palms. "Ruben and Ephram are young adults. I have to check to see if they know something. Or maybe they saw something. You think the snake was left in the early morning hours?"

"It wasn't there when I came down during the night for a glass of water." Sarah got a faraway look in her eyes, and he thought he detected a shudder. "What if whoever left the snake was already in the house watching me get a glass of water? Writing in my journal?"

Nick placed a hand on her arm and had to admit he was surprised when she didn't pull away. "You're fine. I won't let anything happen to you."

"You can't promise that."

"I'll start by finding you someplace else to stay."

Sarah stuck out her lower lip and blew her bangs off her forehead. "I—" she ran her fingers through her bangs "—I haven't decided what I'm going to do." Indecision flashed in her eyes.

Nick tipped his head at Sarah and lifted an eyebrow. "Do you feel safe staying here?"

"Maybe it was a foolish prank." Sarah's voice didn't hold any conviction.

"I wouldn't feel comfortable letting you stay here alone in this house."

"Letting me?" A fiery look descended into her eyes. She shook her head in disgust despite the flicker of fear that swept across her features. This was a woman who had been badly hurt and had trust issues bigger than his.

Nick decided to extend a peace offering for his misstep. "Would you mind coming next door with me? They might be more receptive to talking if I brought along a friendly face." Nick lifted a pleading eyebrow.

"Yeah, throw me under the bus." She pointed to her forehead. "Remember, I'm the reason they got hauled in last night."

"Technically, they were picked up for breaking bottles in the alley." He watched Sarah carefully, waiting for her hard expression to soften.

"At the very least, the Zooks should know that someone broke into your house. They are your neighbors and your landlord. They need to take precautions, too."

"Let's go then. But my money is on Jimmy."

Nick followed Sarah across the lawn to the neighbor's property. A couple young men, their heads covered by straw hats, worked near the barn. Sarah pointed at the closer man. "That's Ephram. And Ruben's over there."

Ephram stopped what he was doing as they approached. Ruben seemed determined to finish his morning chores without interruption.

Nick had been warned when he had started this job about a year ago when he returned from his military service that the Amish were good people, but they didn't take kindly to law enforcement. They liked to handle things within their own community. Having grown up here, Nick already understood this, but he had never worked in the capacity of law enforcement and been directly impacted by their misgivings until recently.

"Morning, men," Nick called, trying to sound friendly. "Could Miss Gardner and I have a word with you?"

"Hello, boys." Sarah smiled. "Ephram, Ruben, this is Deputy Jennings." Ephram and Ruben both looked to be in their late teens, twenty at most.

Ruben stepped forward and crossed his arms, tucking his fingers under his armpits. His eyes moved to the bandage on Sarah's head. "Real sorry to hear you're injured. Good thing Mary Ruth wasn't there. She could have been injured, too." Something about the tight set of his mouth suggested he wasn't happy about Mary Ruth working with Sarah. But Nick couldn't be sure.

"Do you know who was horsing around outside the church? Who might have thrown the rock?"

"We went to the singing," Ruben said. "Mary Ruth was supposed to be there." A hint of annoyance laced his tone. "We were foolish and broke some bottles in the alley. That's all. We weren't near the church."

"Listen," Nick spoke up, "Miss Gardner had more trouble in the early morning hours. Right here at the house on your property."

Ephram stopped shoveling slop into the pigs' troughs and stared at him. "What kind of trouble?" Nick tried to determine if his question was genuine or an act.

Sarah opened her mouth, but before she had a chance to say anything, Nick help up his hand.

He didn't want her to give away details of the crime. Not yet.

"Someone broke into Sarah's house between the hours of four and eight a.m. Did you see anything?"

Ephram glanced down and pushed the dirt around with the toe of his boot. *"Neh."*

"What about you, Ruben?" Sarah asked.

Ruben took off his hat and scrubbed his hand across his blunt-cut hair. His face was clean shaven now, but once he got married, Nick wondered if he'd have enough facial hair to grow a beard. "I overslept this morning."

"And I had to do his chores until he got his sorry self down here."

"No sign of anyone lurking on the porch? Running across the yard? Anything?"

"Neh," they said in unison.

Out of the corner of his eye, Nick noticed their mother crossing the yard to them. "Can we help you?" Temperance seemed more standoffish than she had when she made her way over to Sarah's porch just a little while ago.

"We're trying to determine if your sons saw anything suspicious around my house in the early-morning hours."

Temperance snapped her attention to her nearly grown sons. "This morning? Something happened at the house this morning? Why didn't you tell me when I came over?"

"I didn't want to worry little Patience," Sarah said.

Temperance's lips thinned into a line. "Apple Creek sure has had its share of incidences over the past few years. If you boys saw something, you need to speak up."

"*Neh, Mem,* we didn't see anything," Ruben said.

Temperance smiled tightly at her neighbor. "My boys are *gut* boys. They both have plans to prepare for baptism, and I don't want anything to derail that. Nothing," she added for emphasis. "It makes me wonder if renting that place to an *Englischer* was such a good idea."

All the color seemed to drain from Sarah's face.

Temperance adjusted her bonnet and straightened her shoulders. "I like you, Sarah, and I understand you've fallen on hard times. But my husband decided to rent the house next door against his better wishes. He warned me this was one step closer to inviting the outside world in." She fussed with her apron, obviously uncomfortable with the direction of the conversation. "I had to convince my husband to rent the home to you. Miss Ellinor has always been kind to me. It was a favor. Please don't make me regret my decision."

Out of the corner of his eye, Nick could see Sarah squirming. She was obviously a woman who didn't like conflict.

"That's not my intent," Sarah said, tucking a loose strand of hair behind her ear. "I'm sorry. We'll let you get back to work."

"Sarah," Temperance called, "I know you're doing the work you feel you need to do, but the Amish like to keep things within their own community."

"I understand and respect that," Sarah said. "However, if someone chooses to come to me for help, I will not turn them away. And my intent is not to encourage them to leave the Amish faith, but rather heal within themselves so they can be the best person they can be, whether they choose to be baptized Amish or not."

Temperance seemed to wince. "I like you. I really do. I enjoy having you as a neighbor. But please be careful how you interact with the Amish."

"Do you know something, Mrs. Zook?" Nick asked. Something in her nervous mannerisms made him grow suspicious.

"*Neh.* Not at all. Our family could use the extra finances from the rent, and I'd hate to see Sarah leave…or worse, get hurt."

"I'll see that she's kept safe," Nick said.

Sarah bowed her head, and red splotches appeared on her face.

Suddenly, Mrs. Zook's face lit up. "Perhaps we can let our dog come stay at the house. He makes a pretty good guard dog." The woman was obviously ready to change the subject. "He'd probably lick an attacker to death, but at least his bark would alert you."

"That's not a bad idea." But Nick still felt it advisable for Sarah to move out. She was too isolated out here, even with the Zooks next door. Several hundred feet across a vast field afforded a potential attacker the time and seclusion he needed to do whatever he desired.

Nick tipped his head toward the boys working near the barn. "If your boys remember anything, you'll let me know?" He realized he was grasping at straws. No way would Mrs. Zook contact him.

"They're *gut*," she repeated.

"Even the strongest kids have fallen prey to peer pressure," Nick said evenly.

"Peer pressure out here on the farm is different than whatever you experienced growing up in that big estate on Apple Creek Bluff. You can't relate." She hesitated a fraction. "Nor do we expect you to."

Nick forced a weary smile, deciding he'd

catch the boys another time. Perhaps when he noticed them in town, away from the watchful eye of their parents. "If you see anything suspicious on your property, please let me know."

Temperance lifted her chin and gave him a subtle nod.

When they returned to Sarah's yard, she turned to Nick. "What did Temperance mean about you not being able to relate because of where you grew up?"

He rubbed the back of his neck, debating how much to tell her. Who he was and where he grew up weren't secrets, but it seemed that once people found out he was one of the Jennings who grew up in the huge home sitting on the escarpment in Apple Creek, well, it colored their perception of him. Made them believe he was some rich boy playing at being a cop.

He dropped his arm and smiled. If he wanted Sarah to trust him, he'd have to trust her. "My parents own Jennings Enterprises. They have a lot of money." He left it at that. "I grew up pretty comfortable."

She studied him for a second, then shrugged. "No shame in that, but I can see some people might take issue with it."

"Mostly because they believe I can't relate because I've never struggled with money issues." He supported himself now. He was an adult, but he definitely had a leg up on getting to where he was today.

"What do you make of our conversation with the Zooks?" Nick changed the subject.

"The Zooks are a good family. I'm sure if they saw something, they would have told us." Sarah slowed by the porch. "Temperance is feeling particularly vulnerable. Her sons are right at the age where they'll be making the decision to be baptized and marry and join the Amish community for life. She's undoubtedly afraid they'll get caught up in something that might delay their entrance into the baptismal preparation classes."

Nick rocked back on his heels. "You've picked up on the local customs rather quickly. How long have you been in town?" He felt a smile pulling at the corners of his mouth.

"Six months." She smiled. Her whole face changed when she smiled. He didn't think she could be more attractive. "My job sometimes involves counseling the Amish. Knowing about their culture helps me help them."

Nick nodded.

"I hate dragging a good family into my mess. I don't want to put them in danger." Sarah bit her lip, indecision darkening her eyes.

"They might know something."

"Maybe." She sounded doubtful.

"You really think it's your old boyfriend."

"I'm worried."

"Let me protect you."

"I'd hardly think it's appropriate for me to move in with you. Perhaps I'll take Temperance up on her offer and have their dog keep me company."

It was Nick's turn to smile.

"Let me make a few phone calls. I can send extra patrols out here. What time will you be done with work today?"

"Late afternoon."

"Meet me at the diner for dinner? We can come up with a plan."

"A plan other than packing up and moving again doesn't sound practical." She tipped her head from side to side as if easing out the kinks. "I don't think so."

"You can't keep running."

"I can if I want to live."

FIVE

The memory of the smell of guts and decay made Sarah want to puke. Thankfully, Nick had donned yellow latex kitchen gloves and disposed of the snake before he left.

Gross, gross, triple gross, ran over and over in her head as she scrubbed her kitchen table one more time for good measure, using almost a whole roll of paper towel. She took the garbage and tied it up in a plastic bag. Holding the bag as far away from her body as she could, she pushed through the screen door. She went around the side of the house, dumped it into the trash can. After securing the lid, she glanced around. Awareness prickled her skin.

Relax, you're okay. Even Sarah knew that Jimmy was too much of a coward to attack her in broad daylight. The hallmark of his abuse included keeping it a secret and making everyone question her story. Not his.

She strode back into the house and turned the lock on the door all the same. She said a silent prayer that this lock would be enough. Nick had found one of her windows unlocked, and they assumed this had been the point of entry. Now that it was secured, she should be safe.

Please, Lord, let me be safe.

After Nick had cleaned up the snake, he had bagged the phone for prints. Sarah doubted uncovering the intruder would be that easy.

A little voice in her head, no doubt planted by Jimmy's relentless barbs, told her she had brought all this upon herself. She should have never called her mom last night.

But what about the incident at the church prior to that? What had she done to bring that on?

Nothing. She had done nothing. But she knew what she had to do now. She washed her hands, changed her clothes and headed out on the walk to the center of town to Apple Creek Community Church.

Normally she enjoyed the peaceful stroll along the quiet country road, the solace of it, but today it was too quiet. The wind rustling through the cornstalks lining both sides of the road unnerved her. Nick had told her to call him for a ride, but she needed to do this one thing before she lost her nerve.

And she didn't want Nick to be any more involved than he already was.

She'd have to resign her position at the church and leave Apple Creek.

Run away.

Again.

The memory of the phone call with her mother reverberated in her mind. She couldn't go too far. Her mother wasn't doing well, despite her protests.

The gravel on the berm of the road crunched under her tennis shoes as Sarah picked up her pace. The occasional truck and horse and buggy passed her, but mostly she was alone out here. She hated the feelings of being out of control. Afraid. Unprotected with only cornfields on either side of the road.

Running away to Apple Creek had sent Sarah into a downward spiral, but now—even after all the precautions she had taken—it seemed Jimmy had found her. She fought off the pit of despair that tried to consume her.

The dark emotions reminded her of when her father died. Her world had swirled out of control. Her father had been her protector. Her hero. And then he was gone.

Leaving her and her mother as an incomplete family of two.

After her father's death, she had spent her early adulthood picking the wrong men. Perhaps looking for a father figure. Someone to love her. Someone to protect her. She thought she had found that in Jimmy Braeden. He had been so attentive. Affectionate.

Abusive.

But she didn't realize the latter until it was far too late. Until Jimmy had her in his clutches and wouldn't let go.

The midmorning sun beat hot and steady on her head. She wished she had grabbed a hat before heading out the door. She ran a hand across her forehead. Don't think about it. Keep walking.

It had been next to impossible to leave Buffalo the first time. Now it would be difficult to move again. Sarah had grown accustomed to the quiet, and she'd miss her new friends, however few.

The six months she lived in Apple Creek had been tranquil.

Until yesterday.

Now, with the events of the past twenty-four hours weighing on her shoulders, she arrived at the church. She jogged the last fifty feet, as if a burst of decisiveness wanted to outrun her indecision. And she longed for the wall of air-conditioning she knew would hit her as soon as she opened the door to the church basement.

When Sarah reached the door handle, it made her think of home base in hide-and-seek, a game she had played with the neighborhood kids as a child. They'd run as fast as they could until they threw themselves at the tree, front porch or a square in the cement. Whatever arbitrary location the players had chosen as safe. And then they'd flop over, exhausted, relieved, knowing they were safe and some other sap would be "it." But as an adult, she realized she no longer had a home base.

No place was safe.

Not anymore.

Sarah yanked on the door handle, and the heavy blue door swung open. Pastor Mike had said they were a welcoming church. Locked doors would only create barriers to those who wanted to get closer to God. Or those who were seeking…something.

She slipped inside, and the door slammed behind her and her nerves hummed to life. Anyone could be in the basement meeting room of the church. Yet another reason she had to leave. She'd gather a few of her personal things from her office and then tell Pastor Mike her plans.

Sarah tried not to look at the plywood covering the broken window—had it been some reckless teenagers?

Oh, but what about the snake on my kitchen table?

Either way, she was grateful that someone had cleaned up the mess. She had already dealt with too much this morning. Sarah scrunched her nose, trying to dispel the horrid smell of the dead animal that still lingered, even if only in her memory. Focusing on the task at hand, she emptied a box of hymnals, figuring the pastor wouldn't mind if she used the empty box to pack. She stacked the books neatly on a corner table. As she gathered her personal items, she heard the door open and then after a long silence, click closed. Sarah froze. Her decision to return without her personal protector suddenly didn't seem like a good idea. What would they call her in one of those movies? Too stupid to live?

"Hello."

Sarah's heart soared. Miss Ellinor's voice had never sounded sweeter. "You're in the office early today. I noticed you jogging across the parking lot as if a wild hog was chasing you through the fields. Is everything okay?" Her words floated down the staircase as the older woman gripped the railing and descended each step gingerly.

When she reached the bottom step, Miss Ellinor planted a fist on her hip. "Everything isn't okay. What's going on?"

Sarah stopped putting items into the box. "I was hoping to talk to you and Pastor Mike at the same time."

"He's visiting a church member in the hospital. Poor Mrs. Mann fell and broke a hip."

"I'm sorry to hear that." Sarah admired how the pastor and his wife devoted their lives to their ministry. Helping people as a social worker was the best part of Sarah's job, but lately she wondered how much more she could give to other people before she lost herself entirely.

A pang of guilt pinged her insides. She felt selfish. People in Apple Creek had begun to count on her, and she was ready to run again, leaving them without an advocate when it came to receiving the services they required and deserved.

Let someone else do it. I have my own problems.

Selfish! But dying wasn't going to help anyone.

Miss Ellinor lowered herself into one of the rickety old wooden folding chairs that were probably manufactured circa 1960 and were ubiquitous in church basements. "You're leaving us." It was a statement, not a question.

The look of disappointment on the older woman's face slammed Sarah in the heart. Sarah grabbed a chair and propped it open. She sat next to Miss Ellinor. "I can't thank you and the pastor enough for taking me in. For finding me a place to live. But I'm afraid—" she paused, unwilling to utter his name "—*he* knows where I am. I have to leave. I can't risk anyone getting hurt on account of me."

Miss Ellinor folded her hands in her lap. "I thought the police found a few young men misbehaving in town?"

"They did." Sarah scratched her head and blinked away the image of the snake.

Miss Ellinor pressed her palms together as if she were praying. "Then, there's nothing to worry about. And now that you've gotten to know that nice handsome officer, he can protect you."

Sarah smiled, unwilling to be rude to the woman who had been so kind to her. She didn't want to remind her that her last boyfriend—her current stalker—had been a police officer. And Nick was a deputy sheriff.

"I'm not interested in dating."

Miss Ellinor squared her shoulders and pressed her lips together, the face she often made before she was ready to regale her with a story. "Now, that would be a shame. Nick is such a nice man, and his last girlfriend treated him like dirt. Broke his heart. I'd love to see a girl like you end up with a strong, handsome man like him. A man who treats you right." She quickly shook her head, as if reading Sarah's mind. "He's tough on the outside, but that man has a heart of gold. Do you know his parents are the wealthy folks who have that fancy house up on the hill?" Nick had mentioned something about his parents' wealth.

"Nick could have walked right into his father's business," the pastor's wife continued, "and have a fancy car and all, but he chose to first serve his country and then join the sheriff's department here. Nothing glamorous about that," she added, as if thinking aloud. "Only a good man would make a choice like that when he could have had almost anything he wanted."

Sarah could feel heat and shame pulsing through her veins. Part of her wanted to stop the woman from invading Nick's privacy, the other half—the curious part—wanted to pepper her with a million questions.

Someone broke Nick's heart?

Why didn't he go into the family business?

And he's still single?

Sarah shook the silly thoughts aside. It was

totally none of her business, and poor Nick would probably be embarrassed if he knew Miss Ellinor was spilling his secrets.

A cool knot twisted in her stomach. Had Miss Ellinor ever shared Sarah's secrets? Secrets that could jeopardize her safety?

"I'm not looking for a boyfriend," Sarah said, her common sense winning out over her curiosity. *Certainly not one who is a cop.* "I don't imagine Nick would like us talking about him."

Miss Ellinor waved her hand. "Oh, I'm not being gossipy. All of Apple Creek knows what happened to Nick. That girl was a fool for cheating on him. *And* when he was serving our country. Can you imagine that girl's nerve? Some of the younger generation are so self-involved."

Miss Ellinor leaned forward and pulled Sarah's hands in hers. Tears bit at the back of Sarah's eyes as she stared at their clasped hands. She hadn't realized how separate she had held herself here in Apple Creek. She had missed the simple comforts of a deep friendship. Of course, Sarah had become friendly with Mary Ruth, but out of necessity, Sarah kept a certain distance between them. A tear slipped out of the corner of Sarah's eye and rolled down her cheek.

"Oh, honey, it's okay. Don't cry. What can I do for you?" Miss Ellinor patted her hand.

"I'm a grown woman and I'm crying because

I miss my mom." Her nose tingled and she had to swallow back a knot of emotion. "It's silly, I know."

Miss Ellinor stood and bent over, hugging Sarah. "You aren't silly at all. You've had a rough time of it. Of course you miss your mother. How does she seem in her letters?"

"Her letters are all cheery. She's putting on a brave face." Sarah decided not to get into the prohibited phone call she had made last night. "I'm worried."

"We'll keep her in our prayers." Miss Ellinor patted her back and straightened. "Please don't go. Apple Creek needs you."

Sarah bit her lip, considering. A little part of her wondered if Miss Ellinor had only said that out of pity.

"I do like my work here." She traced the flat edge of the rickety wooden folding chair.

"Then stay." Miss Ellinor held herself with an air of determination. "You're running before you know what's going on. Can you stay until you know you're really in danger from that evil man?" She gave her a knowing glance.

"Even if it's not my former boyfriend, someone's harassing me."

The pastor's wife planted a fist on her hip. "Every time you run into conflict, you're going to run away?" The older woman shook her head.

She pursed her lips, but she had a twinkle in her eye, obviously knowing she was slowly chipping away at Sarah's resolve.

Miss Ellinor pointed to the stairway. "We'll add security features here at the church. We'll lock the doors and make sure you have an escort back and forth from your home."

"But what about the pastor's open-door policy?"

Miss Ellinor waved her hand. "Never hurt a person to knock or ring the bell. Your safety is more important than anything." The older woman patted Sarah's shoulder.

Sarah gave her a sad smile. As much as she appreciated everything Miss Ellinor was willing to do to keep her safe, nothing and no one could protect her from Jimmy if he had a mind to hurt her.

Sarah collapsed into an oversize leather chair in her tiny office in the church basement after her only client for the day left. The hum of the AC unit in the window kept her company. She traced the six-inch tear in the black leather, and her mind drifted.

The client who had just left—she wasn't Amish—had two young children, and although she wouldn't admit it, Sarah suspected she was in an abusive relationship. The young woman wanted to get a divorce, but had no means of support. Sarah promised her that if she really wanted to leave, Sarah would find resources for her.

This was the reason she needed to stay. But could she?

"Are you okay?"

Sarah bolted upright in the chair and swung around. She pressed a hand to her beating chest. "You scared about ten years off my life."

"Sorry, I thought you heard me come in." Mary Ruth smiled sheepishly.

Sarah stood and turned off the AC unit, sending the room into silence, save for Sarah's still-racing heart. She waved her hand. "It's okay."

Her Amish friend turned around and pointed to the box Sarah had left outside her small office. "Are you going somewhere?"

"I was thinking about it."

A thin line creased the young woman's forehead. "Because of what happened here last night?" Mary Ruth leaned back and looked at the boarded-up window. "I feel bad that I wasn't here when it happened."

Sarah shrugged. She was growing tired of being the center of attention. The one thing she enjoyed about Apple Creek was the anonymity. Someone wasn't asking her questions every other minute. Until now.

"It's fine." Then feeling a little embarrassed that she hadn't thought about how this mess had affected Mary Ruth, she asked, "How's Ruben? I hope he's not in too much trouble with his father."

Mary Ruth cocked her head and drew a hand down the long string of her bonnet. "I wouldn't know."

Sarah watched the emotions play across her friend's face. "Aren't you and Ruben getting along?"

Mary Ruth tapped her boot nervously on the doorframe. "I called things off with Ruben."

Sarah made an effort to hide her surprise. "I didn't know." Did last night have something to do with it? Smashing bottles seemed like a minor offense. "Why?"

"It wonders me if I'm not cut out for married life."

Sarah ran her hand over her mouth and gave her next words careful consideration. "Marriage is a huge part of Amish life. If not Ruben, maybe someone else."

Mary Ruth simply raised her shoulders and let them fall. "Maybe."

Sarah thought back to the past few months. Mary Ruth had been spending more and more time helping her. "I appreciate your help here, but maybe it's interfering with your plans to live the Amish way. Maybe you shouldn't have skipped the Sunday singings this past week. You enjoy that time."

"It was easier than facing Ruben," Mary Ruth said, frustration evident in her voice. "He can be very persistent."

Alarm bells clamored in Sarah's head. "He hasn't hurt you, has he?"

Mary Ruth lowered her gaze and shook her head adamantly. *"Neh, neh..."* She slipped into her Pennsylvania Dutch. "He still wants to court me."

"He hasn't accepted the breakup?" Sarah searched the young girl's face.

"He will. He just wants to save face. We hadn't been officially published, nor had he talked to the bishop about marriage, but—" she shrugged again "—people start getting ideas. People talk."

"Do you think it's just a matter of time and he'll move on?" Something about Mary Ruth's hesitation unnerved Sarah. Or maybe she was overly sensitive to boy-girl relationships gone bad.

"Yes, that's it. It's a matter of time."

"Please let me know if I can do anything." Sarah lifted her hands, indicating her small office. "This is my job."

It was Mary Ruth's turn to wave her hand.

"It's nothing as serious as that. Ruben needs to move on. That's all."

Sarah pressed her hands together and studied Mary Ruth. "What are your plans?"

"I admire the work you do. I'd love to be able to help people."

Education beyond the eighth grade was frowned upon in the Amish community. On the farm, there was no need for education beyond the basics. A highly educated Amish person might get ideas. So, it wasn't like Mary Ruth could go to college to become a social worker.

Sarah's pulse beat low and steady in her ears. She swallowed hard. "Are you thinking of leaving the Amish?" Mary Ruth's parents would be devastated, having already lost a son to the outside world. Sarah also realized if her closest Amish friend left the church, it might make Sarah's work in helping the Amish more difficult. Already she was considered an interloper, and if Mary Ruth left, the worst fears of the Amish would be realized.

She was a negative influence.

Sarah shook away the thought. Besides being selfish, did it really matter? Hadn't Sarah decided to leave Apple Creek, anyway?

As if reading her mind, Mary Ruth said, "I have no plans to leave the Amish." She leaned her hip against the doorframe. "But maybe, somehow, I can find a way to help people."

Sarah subconsciously ran a hand across her bandage. "I'm glad you told me. I'll do whatever I can to help you."

Mary Ruth tipped her head toward the box again. "Where are you going?" A frown pulled at the corner of her mouth.

"There's a lot going on right now, and I really don't know what I'm doing."

Mary Ruth levered off the doorframe. "I'm here if you need someone to talk to, too." She smiled.

"Thank you."

"I stopped by to see if you needed help cleaning up the mess, but I see someone already has." Mary Ruth looked around.

"I appreciate it."

"Well, I better go, then. My *mem* needs help with my little sisters so she can run some errands. I told her I'd hurry back. Last time I didn't arrive home on time my *dat* got mad. I don't want him to start telling me I can't come here." Mary Ruth's father worked at a nearby business that manufactured outdoor play sets, allowing—much to his dismay—more freedom for his family to do things away from the farm. Like Mary Ruth helping Sarah. Or like his son getting in with the wrong gang.

"Go then. I'll see you soon."

"Of course." Mary Ruth spun around, her long dress twirling about her.

Sarah leaned back in her large chair and listened to Mary Ruth's footsteps up the stairs. *Why didn't I know Mary Ruth and Ruben were no longer courting?* Sarah must have misread Mary Ruth's hope for the future all wrong. Mary Ruth hadn't been excited about settling into marriage. She had been excited by other possibilities.

Sarah smiled to herself.

Perhaps it was Sarah's turn to learn something from the young Amish girl.

Excited by the possibilities.

Then another thought struck her like a freight train. Mary Ruth's boyfriend suddenly had motive to make Sarah's life miserable.

No, Ruben was a good guy. He had always been pleasant around her. Helpful, even. Well, until his aloofness this morning. But that's to be expected. He was probably still angry about having to go down to the sheriff's station after smashing the bottles.

All indications showed Ruben was a solid young man, intent on living in the Amish way.

Mary Ruth's family might not be too happy with Sarah, either. Her stomach pitched.

Sarah was grasping at straws. It was Jimmy

who was harassing her. It had to be. *Right?*
Sarah winced at the headache forming behind
her eyes.

How could she ever trust herself again to be
a good judge of character?

Outside the church, the late afternoon sun
beat down on Nick. He drew in a deep breath.
After serving overseas in times of war, he'd
never again take for granted the clean scent of
country air, even with its manure undertones.
But fortunately this afternoon, he only caught a
whiff of bundled hay and fresh-cut grass.

Miss Ellinor had called him at the station, encouraging him to check on Sarah when he got
out of work. The pastor's wife had insisted it
wasn't an emergency, but that the "sweet thing"
looked like she could use a friend. Miss Ellinor's phone call had been serendipitous because
Sarah had been reluctant to agree to meet him
at the diner to discuss the next course of action.
Now he had an excuse to see her. He had made
a few phone calls today to a friend in Buffalo,
and Sarah's story didn't seem to add up.

Nick didn't like secrets.

He slammed his truck door shut and spun
around at the sound of gravel crunching under
footsteps. He wasn't partial to surprises, either.

Miss Ellinor lifted a picnic basket by the handle and smiled, by way of explanation. "I had some leftovers, and I thought you and Sarah might like a nice picnic. Down by the lake maybe?"

Nick shook his head and smiled. "You're incorrigible. I'm guessing Sarah didn't really look like she could use a friend."

"Oh, no, she looks like she could use a friend, especially a handsome young friend like yourself." She smiled coyly and without a hint of apology.

"I'm not as young as you might think." He ran a hand across his scratchy beard.

"All the more reason to get you settled down."

Nick slowly shook his head but couldn't stop the smile from spreading across his face. He wasn't interested in getting involved with someone. Especially not with someone who seemed to be harboring as many secrets as the last woman he had gotten involved with. He had seen firsthand the destruction secrets had on a solid relationship. Never mind trying to build a relationship on the shaky foundation of skeletons in a closet.

The side door of the church swung open and Sarah stepped out clutching her large bag. She seemed to startle a minute when her gaze landed on Nick. She composed herself and made her way over to where he and Miss Ellinor stood.

"Um…" Her gaze drifted from Nick to the picnic basket in Miss Ellinor's hand and back to Nick. "Did we have plans?"

"I'll leave this picnic basket here," Miss Ellinor said as she placed it in the bed of Nick's truck. "I went through a lot of effort, I wouldn't want it to go to waste."

"Thank you." Nick didn't take his eyes off Sarah, who narrowed her gaze.

"What's this about?"

"Miss Ellinor called me and told me to come check on you."

Sarah raised a skeptical eyebrow.

"But apparently it was a ruse to send us off on a picnic." Nick walked around to the back of his pickup truck and lifted one side of the picnic basket. The items were neatly secured, but he could smell the fresh bread and a hint of egg and onion. "Oh, man, I think she made us her famous potato salad." Nick wasn't the kind to attend church, but as a deputy sheriff, he had the occasion to sample Miss Ellinor's cooking at the annual church outing. Most of the town attended, even the Amish, so he never felt out of place despite his lack of Sunday church attendance.

"Potato salad?" Sarah shook her head, smiling. "I suppose it would be a shame to let it go to waste."

"We need to eat, right?"

"We do." Sarah surprisingly seemed down-right agreeable. Or maybe she was hungry.

Once they were settled in his truck, Nick turned to her. "Should we have a picnic by the lake?"

Sarah shoved her oversize bag down next to her legs. "That's fine."

He turned out onto the road and decided he needed to get a few things off his chest before they reached the lake. Maybe then they could relax and enjoy their meal.

"I made a few phone calls this morning."

"Phone calls?" He could hear the trepidation in her tone. "In regards to me?"

"I have a friend who's a private investigator in Buffalo."

"What did you do?" Her voice was barely above a whisper, but it held tremendous re-straint. "I've been hiding in Apple Creek for six months, keeping all my communication with my mother carefully orchestrated, and then I meet you. Now, you up and call a friend? An inves-tigator whose questions will likely raise more questions. About me!" Her voice grew high-pitched. "Take me home."

"Please, we need to talk." A muscle worked in his jaw.

Sarah shifted in her seat and said what was

really on her mind, "What if the two incidents weren't Jimmy? Now you've drawn him a map to my front door. He'll find me for sure."

"My friend can be trusted."

"I need to know everything you said. I need to know who he talked to." Sarah turned to face him, and he gave her a sideways glance. The distrust in her eyes cut him to the core.

Sarah watched the cornfields roll by as Nick drove along the country road. She clamped her jaw shut, seething at his audacity at calling a private investigator about her situation.

"I asked him to quietly look into Jimmy Braeden," Nick said, his voice holding a hint of an apology. "Check out his work schedule. See if he could find out what the man was up to without drawing any attention to himself... or more importantly, *you*."

"You shouldn't have." Sarah closed her eyes and sank into the seat. Nick had no right to contact anyone in Buffalo on her behalf. She could only imagine what Nick had said about her. Her ears grew hot at the thought of people talking about her, discussing her situation.

"By all accounts, Officer Braeden is a good guy." Nick's comment was like a knife to the heart.

"Do you think I'm lying?"

"I'm trying to uncover the truth."

"I don't lie." Sarah fisted her hands in her lap as he slowed the truck and turned into a gravel lot. "Why would I make up a story about an abusive boyfriend?"

Nick cut her a sideways glance. "You have no reason to."

Sarah wasn't sure if he meant it or if he was saying it to appease her. *Why had she agreed to come on a picnic with him?*

"Can we please enjoy this meal Miss Ellinor made for us? Call a truce for the next hour?" Nick sounded so sincere.

Sarah turned and looked out over the water. The afternoon sun was glittering on the lake. It was beautiful. She found some of the anxiety ebbing away. Not all of it, but some. She figured just enough to allow her to hold a civil conversation and maybe enjoy the picnic Miss Ellinor had taken the time to prepare.

Without waiting for an answer, Nick hopped out of the vehicle and went around and opened the door for her. Jimmy had long ago stopped making her feel special by performing simple courtesies. Like opening a car door.

Nick smiled at her, one that seemed to be asking for forgiveness. She wished it was as easy as that and this was simply a nice first date between two single people in Apple Creek, but her life had taken too many twists and turns over the years to let her guard down.

Besides, she wasn't staying in Apple Creek. Not long term anyway.

And she wasn't interested in dating. Not a cop. Not Nick.

He grabbed the picnic basket and headed toward the water's edge. She was surprised no one else was out enjoying the park.

He set the basket down and opened one side and pulled out a red-and-white-checkered blanket.

"Looks like Miss Ellinor thought of everything," Nick said as he spread the blanket on the grass. He plopped down on it and seemed unconcerned that Sarah was standing there watching him.

"She's a wonderful cook."

Nick laughed. "And apparently a matchmaker." He shrugged. "I suppose it's not that unusual. As a pastor's wife, she must meet a lot of people who have things in common."

"Do we?" Sarah asked, unable to keep the sarcasm from her tone.

He pulled out a cold bottle of water and handed it to her. "I'd like to think so." He squinted up at her and smiled, a smile that reached his warm brown eyes. She accepted the bottle and dropped to her knees on the blanket.

Nick pulled out potato salad in two plastic containers, a bag of chips and individually wrapped sandwiches.

Sarah's stomach growled. "I've been so busy all day, I didn't realize how hungry I was." She pulled back the plastic wrap covering hers and took a bite of the chicken-salad sandwich. "Wow, this is really good."

They ate in silence for a few minutes until Nick spoke. "Now about those phone calls I made…"

Sarah's adrenaline spiked, and she lowered her sandwich. "Has it already been an hour? Remember our truce?"

Nick lifted an eyebrow as if to say, "You didn't actually think we could avoid the elephant in the room?"

Sarah maneuvered her legs from a kneeling position to a more comfortable sitting position. Her feet tingled from lack of circulation. "You know how to ruin a girl's appetite." She held her breath, waiting, anxious to know if his phone calls had uncovered anything.

"Matt, the private investigator, and I served together in the army."

Sarah moved her potato salad around with her fork. "Jimmy has a lot of friends, and he's *very* convincing." Already she felt defensive.

"You're right. Jimmy claims you were fired from your last job and were forced to move away."

"He's lying."

"I know." Nick reached across and touched her knee. She was too weary to pull away.

"What if your friend's inquiries cause me more problems?"

"We can trust my friend Matt. He's a good guy. He's smart. He won't say anything to put you in jeopardy."

Sarah bowed her head and studied the blanket.

"Can you trust me on this?"

She slowly looked up, and a pang of regret zinged her heart when she saw the despondent look on his face.

"I hardly know you."

"Hear me out. Matt made a call to one of his friends at Orchard Gardens police headquarters and discreetly checked the work rosters. James Braeden was working last night."

Her mouth immediately went dry. "Jimmy normally works the day shift."

"He apparently worked a few doubles recently. Maybe there's something going on at work?"

"Are you saying he couldn't have been harassing me because he was at work?" She felt the knot easing between her shoulder blades.

"It would seem that way."

Sarah nodded, letting what he said sink in. "That means someone else smashed the window and left the snake on my kitchen table." But for some strange reason, a stranger harassing her seemed less threatening than Jimmy.

Sarah bowed her head and tucked a strand of hair behind her ear. "That jibes with something else I learned today." She looked up and met his encouraging gaze. "Mary Ruth told me she broke up with Ruben. Maybe he blames my influence for the demise of his relationship."

Nick nodded. "Maybe. What about her family? They would be upset, too. Baptism and marriage are important milestones in the Amish community. I understand Mary Ruth's older brother recently moved away."

Sarah had yet to meet Mary Ruth's family. It was almost like the young woman was working hard to keep the parts of her life separate. Considering their different backgrounds, Sarah understood that, but did that also mean she had a very angry family member at home who might blame Sarah for the perceived influence she had over Mary Ruth, especially in light of her brother jumping the fence?

Sarah dragged her fingers through her hair. "I wish my job came with a training manual, sometimes."

Nick wiped his mouth with a napkin. "I'll do some digging."

Sarah reached out and clasped his wrist. "Don't make it obvious. I have a tough enough time getting the few Amish who do come to me for help to trust me. I don't want them to think they no longer can."

"I understand." He tilted his head to look deeply in her eyes. "Can *you* trust *me*?"

Sarah nodded. She could. She had to.

"There's something else." Nick bent his knee in front of him and rested his elbow on it and stared over the lake, giving Sarah the opportunity to study his strong profile.

If only they had met under different circumstances...

"I had Matt do a welfare check on your mother."

Sarah's heart skipped a beat. She was unsure if she should be mad or grateful. Right now, she chose to be grateful.

"How is she?" The world seemed to slow down as she held her breath and waited for a response.

Nick slowly turned to look at her. "He's never met your mom before, but he thought perhaps she wasn't doing well. The house was a mess and—"

"My mother always kept a meticulous house."

Suddenly the chicken sandwich didn't sit so well in her stomach. Her mind drifted to the conversation last night. Her mother's persistent cough. All Sarah's doubts and regrets overwhelmed her.

Maybe Sarah shouldn't have left Buffalo.

Sarah closed her eyes. "What am I going to do?"

"I'll help you. However I can." Nick's compassionate words washed over her. "But I don't know if it's safe to visit her. That's what you're thinking, right?"

Tears burned the back of her eyes, and she struggled to find the words. What could she say? "You have to understand how hard it is to be away from my mom at this time."

His intense scrutiny unnerved her, so she redirected the conversation. "Are you close with your parents?"

Nick laughed. "Well, my parents are a little different. They're entrepreneurs and they travel the world. Work has always been their first priority, but they always made sure we had everything we needed. And they're very generous in the community."

Curiosity piqued her interest. "How did both you and your sister end up in Apple Creek?"

"When we were little, my parents wanted to get away from the city. They needed a quiet place to think. Since they owned their own business…well, *businesses* now, they could live anywhere. We moved from Buffalo to Apple Creek when I was around seven."

"You didn't follow them into the family business?"

Nick shook his head. "It never appealed to me. I wanted to do something more concrete. To help people."

"And your sister became a doctor in a health-care clinic. Interesting."

"Yes, and my parents see to it that the clinic is fully funded."

"Wow." Sarah took a sip of water. The soft breeze against her skin felt wonderful.

"Oh, but I have another sister. She went to school for accounting and she's very successful, running one arm of the family business." Nick got a faraway look in his eyes. "The lifestyle never interested me. My parents were always gone. I was raised more by the nanny than my parents." He waved his hand in dismissal.

"Trust me, growing up with a lot of money in a big house in the country wasn't a hardship. But when the time came, I wanted to go in a different direction careerwise. My parents were always supportive in the way they knew how. They paid for my college and they support the clinic." There was something lonely in his eyes that Sarah could relate to.

Sarah took another long drink of water. "What am I going to do about my mom? I'm hiding in Apple Creek to stay safe, but I won't be able to live with myself if my mom dies alone." Her voice cracked over the word *dies*.

Nick reached out and covered her hand. "Then I think *we* should pay her a visit."

Fear washed over her, and her anxiety made her stomach knot. "I promised my mother I'd stay safe."

"I'll keep you safe." The conviction and sincerity in his eyes warmed her heart. "You can't run away."

"I don't know…"

"*Can* you trust me?" He asked her yet again. He squeezed her hand.

Sarah had no reason not to trust him, but she had been wrong in her assessment of people before.

But what choice did she have? She nodded and turned to face him. They locked gazes. Sarah found herself hypnotized by his kind eyes. Before her brain engaged and she nipped her heart's impulse, she leaned in at the same time Nick did. His soft lips covered hers, a fleeting kiss full of promise. He pulled away and a light glistened in his eyes.

"I won't let you down." A small smile played on his lips.

A million emotions tangled inside her. Sarah shifted and turned her focus to the sparkling lake and let out a long sigh.

Dear Lord, I need Your guidance on this one. Can I trust this man?

SIX

On the drive home from their picnic at the lake, Sarah tried to sift through her conflicted feelings of despair, uncertainty and a new emotion: hope. Could she trust Nick to protect her secret? To protect her? Could they really go visit her mom?

Her swirling thoughts created overwhelming anxiety that nearly consumed her by the time they reached her house. Sarah was about to tell Nick to forget their plans of checking on her mother in Buffalo—it was too risky—when she noticed Mary Ruth sitting on her front porch. Her bonneted head leaned in close to a dog, a golden retriever. He must belong to the Zooks. Mary Ruth stroked his soft fur and seemed to be lost in thought.

Nick noticed the Amish girl at the same time Sarah did. "Mary Ruth, right?"

"Yeah, she usually visits me at the church. I wonder why she's here. I saw her earlier today."

"Do you want me to come with you to talk to her?"

Sarah slowly shook her head. "No, if something's wrong, she's more likely to open up to me when I'm alone." She cut a sideways glance to Nick. "No offense."

"None taken." Sarah was still trying to adjust to his easy manner. "Think about that trip to Buffalo. I could take you later this week."

"Are you sure that's a good idea?" Sarah's stomach dropped. *Can I really visit my mom?*

"Yes. You'll be fine. You can wear something nondescript," Nick continued. "Do you have a baseball cap?"

She couldn't help but smile. Nick sounded like he was planning a bank heist. Not a trip to her childhood home. "I might be able to find a cap."

"Great." Nick turned to face her, and a light twinkled in his eyes. He reached out and covered her hand with his, and the warmth spread up her arm and coiled around her heart.

Heat warmed her cheeks, and once again she wished their circumstances had been different. She couldn't allow herself to be caught up with another charming guy.

Especially not another cop.

Sarah might be willing to trust Nick to keep her safe, *for now.* But she couldn't trust her heart to him.

Then why did I kiss him by the lake?

Sarah pulled her hand out from under his. "Later this week we'll go to Buffalo. Visit my mom. But we can't tell her ahead of time. I'd hate for her to tell someone in her excitement." She forced a confidence into her voice that she didn't feel. She climbed out of the truck and walked slowly toward the front porch. Mary Ruth didn't get up to greet her; instead she seemed to be holding tighter onto the dog's collar as his tail whacked the young girl's shoulder when it stood and barked, enthusiastically greeting Sarah.

"Is this my guard dog the Zooks promised?"

"Yes, Mrs. Zook walked him over while I was waiting for you. I didn't have the heart to tell her you were leaving. And she didn't seem to want to stick around to talk to me."

"Temperance knows about you and Ruben?"

"I suppose *everyone* knows about me and Ruben."

"Word really does spread quickly in a small town." Sarah leaned a hip on the porch railing. She studied Mary Ruth. While most girls her age back home were experimenting with makeup and fashion, Mary Ruth looked fresh and cute in her bonnet and makeup-free face.

Such innocence. Yet underneath lay such turmoil.

"I had to come by. I couldn't get the fact that

you're leaving out of my head. I hope you'll reconsider." Mary Ruth swiped at a tear. "You can't run away like my brother."

Sarah bit her tongue, not wanting to disappoint her friend further, but also unable to lie. Sarah had no idea how much longer she could stay in Apple Creek.

"Mary Ruth, you're stronger than you think." The young woman needed to know that, for many reasons. Mary Ruth needed the confidence to face her parents, Ruben, the bishop, her community if she hoped to find peace in her life.

Mary Ruth hitched a shoulder. The dog licked the Amish girl's cheek, sensing her need for comfort.

The conversation Sarah and Nick had had by the lake flitted in her brain like a fly trying to make its escape out the closed window and bouncing off the screen. "Does your family know you've called off your courtship with Ruben?"

"*Yah*, my *dat* was asking a lot of questions about if I'd be joining the next baptismal class." An Amish person was baptized prior to marriage.

Sarah sat next to her young friend. She wanted to put her hand on her back, but she didn't know how well it would be received. The Amish weren't big on outward displays of affection.

"I have all these decisions to make, and I'm scared and confused," Mary Ruth whispered. "My parents expect so much of me since my brother left. They're worried. It's every Amish parent's wish that their children stay in the community."

Sarah knew that overwhelmingly, the young Amish did remain, which explained the growing numbers of Amish. Sarah supposed it was easier to commit to the familiar than make the bold move to leave home, often forever.

The dog walked over Mary Ruth's lap and wedged himself between the two women and put his head down on Sarah's lap. She ran her hand absentmindedly down the smooth fur of his head.

"Take it as it comes. You're young. You have time to figure it out. If you don't join the next baptismal class, you can join the one after that." It would be worse if Mary Ruth were baptized and then decided to leave. Baptism was a forever commitment. If she left after baptism, she'd be shunned.

"They're worried I'll be a negative influence on my siblings. They want me to hurry up and commit for fear I won't ever."

The stalks of corn rustled in the wind in the

nearby field. All these months Sarah had gotten to know Mary Ruth, she thought the young girl was steadfast in her determination to be baptized into the Amish community and then be married. Turned out no one ever knows what was truly in another person's heart.

"Did something else happen? Besides your brother leaving?" Sarah pivoted, and the dog shoved his snout under Sarah's chin and she couldn't help but smile and pat his head. *Some guard dog.* "You know, your brother may find his way back. Don't give up hope. And please, don't make a lifetime decision because you're afraid of disappointing your parents. You have to reach in deep and do what you feel God is calling you to in your heart." Sarah had always been careful not to sway an Amish person against their way of life, but she sensed Mary Ruth's struggle was real. The poor girl had to find her place in the world.

A pink flush crept up Mary Ruth's face. "You think differently than I've been taught. The Amish are more community driven. It's not supposed to be about what I want."

Sarah grabbed the railing and stood. The dog jumped up, perhaps thinking they were going for a walk. "I'd never try and convince you to leave the Amish community. I'm just asking that you dig deep and try to envision the life that's best suited for you."

Mary Ruth stood and swiped at the back of her long skirt. "Please don't leave Apple Creek."

Sarah hated to disappoint her friend, but she couldn't lie to her, either. She didn't know what her next step was.

Sarah rubbed the dog's head, and he leaned into her leg. She laughed, shaking her head. "Do the Zooks really think this dog—what's his name? Buddy?—will make a good guard dog?"

Mary Ruth laughed. "He barks every time a stranger comes up. What more do you need?"

"Can you do me a favor?" Sarah asked as she stroked the dog's fur. "Can you take the dog back over to the Zooks? Tell them I'll be happy to have him come back, maybe in a few days." She didn't want to worry about Buddy when she and Nick took their trip into Buffalo.

Mary Ruth's mouth formed into a perfect O.

"You can't keep avoiding Ruben. It's a small town." And maybe some of the hard feelings would go away if Ruben and Mary Ruth had a chance to talk.

The image of the dismembered snake flashed in her mind. Could Ruben be that angry? No, that had all the markings of Jimmy. Mary Ruth stomped down the steps, her posture resigned. At the bottom of the steps, she turned around and faced Sarah. "You always give me advice, but can I give you some?"

Sarah raised her eyebrows and held out her hand as if to say, "Go ahead."

"You deserve happiness, too."

Not sure what to say, Sarah plastered on a false smile. Sarah made her life's work about helping others without revealing much about herself.

"You help people like me, but you seem sad and lonely." Mary Ruth absentmindedly reached for Buddy as he jumped around the folds of her long dress, eager for attention, lightening the mood.

Sarah smiled. "Buddy wants to play."

Mary Ruth crouched down and patted the dog's head. "He makes it hard to have a serious discussion."

"I know." Sarah crossed her arms and grew solemn. "I can't share why I'm in Apple Creek, but I'm learning to trust Nick." She wasn't sure why she shared this information, but she supposed she didn't want her young Amish friend to worry.

It was Mary Ruth's turn to raise her eyebrows. "So, it's Nick now." She beamed. "You're not leaving?" Her hopeful tone buoyed Sarah.

"Not yet."

"*Gut.*" Mary Ruth said.

"And Mary Ruth… Don't feel you need someone else to make you happy. Find happiness within yourself." This had been a mantra Sarah repeated to herself often. She understood the Amish way wasn't to pursue personal goals, but rather work for the community, but she wanted her friend to make this very serious choice about baptism and marriage from a place of strength and not out of desperation, need or loneliness.

"I'll do my best."

Sarah watched Mary Ruth cross the yard. Sarah's heart started pounding when she noticed Ruben cutting across the property to meet her at the fence. Sarah lifted her hand to wave, but he turned his back to her without waving back. He must not have seen her.

Or maybe he really was angry with her.

The fluttery feelings in Sarah's stomach had only intensified over the past few days, a mixture of excitement and pure dread. Now the day had come, and she and Nick were headed to Buffalo to visit her mom. All had been quiet in Apple Creek since the snake incident—perhaps the increased sheriff's patrols by her rented house had been a deterrent—but Sarah couldn't help but feel like going to Buffalo was poking a hornet's nest.

"You haven't been home in six months?" Nick

merged the sleek compact car onto the road after stopping at her mother's favorite bakery to pick up some pastry hearts. He had borrowed it from his parents' fleet of executive vehicles that were registered in Buffalo, not Apple Creek, one of the many precautions they had taken. The other was leaving after nightfall.

"No, I haven't been back." Sarah threaded her fingers and twisted her hands. "At the next light turn right." At this hour, she envisioned her mother sitting in her favorite recliner watching whatever police drama was running on cable. She had tried to show her mother how to use Netflix so she could binge-watch her favorite shows whenever she wanted, but all the controls and choices were too much for her. Her mother liked things simple.

Sarah laughed to herself. Her mother had always made the best of things, until cancer and Jimmy Braeden infected their lives. Some things were too hard to overcome. Sarah hoped her surprise visit didn't negatively affect her mom, making it even harder for her mom once she had left again.

Oh, maybe this isn't a good idea.

As they approached her old neighborhood in Buffalo, Sarah's nerves vibrated with anticipation. She longed to see Mom, but she couldn't shake the foreboding that something bad was going to happen—*really* bad. Ever since Sarah's panic attacks started, she struggled to separate real danger from perceived danger.

She sent up a silent prayer that her fight-or-flight response was off-kilter considering she was home for the first time in half a year.

"I live—my mom lives," she corrected herself, "on this street about ten houses in on the left."

Nick must have sensed her unease. "Everything is going to be all right. This car is registered to my parents' company, which has a Buffalo address. It would take a huge leap to connect it to Apple Creek and you, for that matter."

"So, remind me of this great plan." Sarah's tone came off as sarcastic, but inside she was trembling and nauseous. She prayed she'd be strong for Mom. And she prayed her mom was doing better than Nick's friend had led her to believe. Matt didn't know her mother, so what basis did he have to make that call?

That's the lie she had been telling herself since Nick had suggested they visit her mom. And what she was quickly learning about Nick, when he made a decision, he didn't waste time putting it into action.

"We'll park on the street a house away so as not to draw attention."

"What if someone sees me?" Sarah's legs started to shake, and she couldn't stop them.

"Did you bring a hat?"

Sarah nodded and pulled out a university baseball cap. It had her college logo on it, a large public university where she'd earned her master's degree. She couldn't recall ever having worn it. She looked goofy in hats.

"Tuck your hair up in it."

Sarah did as Nick had instructed as he came to a stop at the light at the corner of her street. Nostalgia bit at her insides when she remembered how many times she used to ride her bike around the block in this neighborhood. How she and her friends would make a hopscotch board with chalk or play on the shuffleboard court painted on her best friend's driveway.

All a lifetime ago.

The light turned green, and the car in front of them proceeded through the intersection, allowing Nick to turn right onto her street.

Sarah's heart plummeted and her mouth went dry. Rescue vehicles were parked near the house. Sarah couldn't find any words. *Are they here for my mom? No, no, no...*

Nick reached across and touched her hand, sensing her unease. He parked across the street and down two houses. Sarah stared at the fire truck on the street and the ambulance in her mother's driveway. Her stomach knotted, and she feared she was going to throw up.

"My mom," she whispered, her voice hoarse with emotion. She pushed open the door and climbed out, her legs unsteady under her.

Nick scrambled out of the car and jogged around to her side and grabbed her elbow. "It's okay. Let's go in and see what's going on."

Unable to speak around the lump in her throat, Sarah nodded. *Please don't be dead. Please don't be dead.* Then she closed her eyes and prayed in earnest. *Dear Lord, watch over my mom. Let her be okay. Let me be able to see her again.*

"Are you okay?" Sarah opened her eyes to find Nick close to her, studying her face.

"I need to see my mom."

"Come on. I'll be right there with you." He took her elbow. Sarah turned toward the house and noticed the outline of a man in her mother's doorway.

Broad shoulders. Thick chest. Flat buzz cut. *Jimmy.*

It couldn't be.

It had to be. She'd recognize his stance anywhere.

Sarah yanked away from Nick's touch, her world tipping off its axis. She flattened her hand against the cool metal of the passenger window and ducked her head.

"It's him," Sarah whispered. "Jimmy Braeden is standing in my mother's foyer."

At the alarmed expression on Sarah's face, Nick's gaze snapped to the front door. A tall, broad-shouldered police officer stood in the doorway. Nick couldn't be certain if the man was watching them or the EMTs loading the ambulance.

"Are you sure it's him?"

From her semicrouched position, Sarah glanced over the roof of the car. "Yes." She visibly shuddered. "It's him. I'm sure. I don't know why he's here. He's not a Buffalo cop. He's in a neighboring suburb."

Nick gently took Sarah's trembling hand. His heart shattered for her. "You're safe. I'm here." She looked up at him, and her eyes glistened under the white glow of the moonlight. Sarah nodded slightly. Unsure. He hated that a man had done this to her. Made her afraid. He tamped down his anger. He had to keep calm if he didn't want to raise any red flags.

"Get inside the car and lock the doors. Stay low. I'll be right back."

Sarah stared at him, uncertainty flickering

across her face. "Don't leave me here on the street. Alone."

"It'll be okay. Lock the doors," he repeated. "We need to see what's going on with your mom."

Sarah spun around and clutched his arm. "Let's follow the ambulance to the hospital. Don't waste time talking to him."

"Sarah, trust me." Nick brushed his thumb across her cheek, and she leaned into his touch. "I won't jeopardize your safety."

Sarah nodded slightly and slipped into the car. Nick handed her the keys. "Stay in the car. Don't get out no matter what. And if things go south, drive away."

She opened her mouth to protest. Nick locked gazes with her. *Trust me.*

Wide-eyed, Sarah nodded in silent agreement. He trusted she wouldn't leave the car. He straightened and placed a hand on the doorframe. "Hand me the bakery bag."

Sarah twisted around and grabbed the bag from the floor in the back of the car.

Nick watched the man still standing in the doorway. "What church does your mom belong to?"

"Saint Al's?" Sarah answered, a question in her voice.

"Okay…now lock the doors as soon as I close the door."

Sarah nodded ever so slightly. Nick closed the door and heard the click of the automatic locks. He crossed the street with the bakery bag in hand. He glanced over his shoulder at the car. In the darkness, Sarah wasn't visible inside. Nick made a straight line toward the ambulance, but the man who had been standing in the doorway strode out to the driveway and cut him off.

The man matched the image of Officer James Braeden that Nick had pulled up on the Orchard Gardens Police website.

"Can I help you?" Jimmy asked, his eyes piercing and dark. Anger and entitlement rolled off him in waves.

Nick tamped down his growing dislike for the man, afraid it would show on his face. He relaxed his shoulders and tried to act like he wasn't former military or current law enforcement. Nonthreatening.

"Is that Mrs. Gardner? Is she okay?" Nick put on an air of concern consistent with being a long-time friend.

"And you are?" Jimmy asked, not offering any information. Nick wondered why he was here when he wasn't a Buffalo cop.

"Oh, I'm sorry." Nick held out his free hand, offering to shake the man's hand. "I'm Nick—"

he purposely didn't give a last name, even a fake one. Harder for the officer to catch him in a lie. "My mother and Mrs. Gardner are friends from St. Al's. My mother wanted Mrs. Gardner to have these baked goods." Nick lifted up the bag as evidence. "Thought they'd cheer her up. But now I see she's taken a turn for the worse." Nick turned toward the street and noticed the taillights of the ambulance disappear. He knew Sarah must be going out of her mind stuck inside the car, wondering what was going on with her mother.

With Jimmy.

Nick hoped she took comfort in seeing the ambulance didn't have on its lights and siren. That had to be an encouraging sign.

Unless she suspected there was no longer any sense of urgency.

Nick turned back around and found Jimmy staring at him, the two men squaring off eye to eye. "As you can see, Mrs. Gardner has been taken to the hospital."

"Did she call the ambulance?" Nick asked, trying to glean some information to share with Sarah.

"A neighbor did. Happened to stop by to check on her. When Mrs. Gardner didn't answer, she peered through the window and found the old lady flat on the floor. Unconscious."

Jimmy looked past him to his vehicle parked in the street. Nick had purposely made sure he didn't park under a streetlamp so as not to draw attention to the details of the car. Now, he was especially glad because Sarah was nothing more than a shadow.

"My mother's a friend. She'll be concerned. Is there any news I can give her?"

"They're taking her to Buffalo Mercy."

"Did she regain consciousness?"

"Yes, but she's confused." Jimmy turned his focus to Nick's car. "Is someone waiting in the car?"

Nick lifted a hand, he tried to act casual, but he was on high alert. "My wife. We're on our way out tonight. Once she saw the ambulance, we knew we wouldn't be visiting with Mrs. Gardner." Nick frowned. "I suppose I won't be leaving these baked goods. Any chance anyone else in the house would enjoy them?"

"If you knew Mrs. Gardner, then you'd know she only has one daughter. She's currently out of town." The tight set of Jimmy's mouth must have been his "I'm annoyed with the world" tell.

"It's my mother who likes to visit with her friends after church. Me, I'm more a get in and get out and I'm good for another week." Nick shrugged. "Just hope lightning doesn't strike me dead while I'm there."

Behind Jimmy in the house, Nick heard a Buffalo police officer instructing another officer to make sure the house was secure before they left.

"It's a shame her daughter is out of town. Has someone contacted her? Let her know her mother has fallen ill?" Nick let the question hang out there.

Jimmy scrubbed a hand across his cropped hair as he studied Nick. Nick had to resist the urge not to put this guy in his place. He didn't want to trigger Jimmy's temper.

"Someone from our department will be sure to track her down," the Buffalo cop said.

Nick nodded curtly. "Night." Nick made eye contact with the Buffalo cop and then Jimmy. Nick turned and jogged across the lawn. He waited until Jimmy climbed into a large SUV parked in front of Mrs. Gardner's house and pulled away. He didn't want to open the car door and allow the dome light to reveal his passenger.

In the briefest of seconds before he pulled his door shut and the dome light went dark, he saw tears shining on Sarah's pretty face. His heart went out to her.

Given a chance, he'd punch old Jimmy in the jaw. No man had the right to treat a woman as poorly as he had treated Sarah. Now she had lost time with her mother.

He hoped they weren't too late.

Undoubtedly, Sarah would insist they go to the hospital to check on her mother. Given the circumstances, he couldn't deny her.

He only hoped he could protect her.

SEVEN

Sarah and Nick waited two hours and then entered the hospital through the emergency-room doors. Under normal circumstances, Sarah would have never hoped for a busy ER when her mother was somewhere inside awaiting treatment. The crowded waiting room allowed her and Nick to slip in relatively unnoticed by the busy medical staff once Nick and she got past security with a flick of his badge. The wait was excruciating, but they had hoped the initial chaos of her mother's arrival—and the chance of running into Jimmy—had gone down exponentially.

Sarah had worked at this hospital a few years back as an intern in social work. She was familiar with the layout of the ER. She showed Nick a photo from her wallet of her mother. Separately, they each traveled down each side of the long hallway of examination rooms. When she spotted her mom in the last room, her heart stopped and her vision narrowed.

Sarah stared at her mother through the glass on the top half of the door. Her mother looked old and frail under the white sheet. Her face sunken. Her skin papery white. Her eyes closed. Tears blurred Sarah's vision, and she quickly swiped at them. She had to be strong.

Sarah glanced over at Nick, and he had just turned from looking in the last room on his side of the hallway. She nodded to him. Concern flashed in his eyes. He hustled across the hall to her and put a comforting hand on the small of her back. He didn't say anything. He didn't have to.

"I wonder if a doctor can answer any of our questions?" Sarah whispered.

"I'll find one. You go in and see your mother."

She nodded, suddenly feeling like the little girl who visited her dad one last time in the emergency room the night of his accident. She shoved the thought aside and pushed open the door. Her mother didn't move. Cold fear pulsed through her veins. What if this was the end?

Dear Lord, please don't let this be the end. I'm not ready. I need more time. Please watch over her.

Sarah moved to her mother's side. She took off her baseball cap and set it down on the edge of the bed, letting her long blond hair cascade over her shoulders. She felt ridiculous in the cap, but understood she needed to hide her identity.

As an afterthought, she glanced around the room, hoping there weren't security cameras and then decided for once she was going to put Jimmy out of her mind.

Dismissing her plight—she felt selfish at times—she took her mother's smooth, cool hand in her own. She studied her mother's wedding rings, something she hadn't taken off even though she had been a widow longer than she had been married.

"Mom," she whispered, emotion clogging her throat, "I love you."

"Love you, too," came her mother's quiet, raspy reply.

Sarah's eyes flashed to her mother's face. Her eyes were still closed, but her mother squeezed her daughter's hand. A faint squeeze, but a response all the same. A tear trickled down Sarah's face.

"How do you feel, Mom?" Sarah glanced toward the door, hoping Nick would reappear with a doctor or nurse to answer her questions.

Her mother pried her eyes open a slant. "Oh, the light is bright."

Sarah glanced around, but didn't see a switch. Since this was the ER and not a private room, she figured her mother would have to deal with the lights. "I'm sorry." She smoothed her mother's hair off her forehead. "What happened?"

Her mother's forehead creased. "I don't remember…"

"Don't worry. You're getting care now."

"How did you know I was in the hospital? Who called you?"

Sarah smiled. "Even sick, you don't miss a beat, do you, Mom?"

A thin smile curved her mother's lips.

"I snuck back home to see you. Good thing, too."

"I didn't mean to worry you. Is it safe for you to be here?" Her mother examined Sarah and noticed the bandage. "Your forehead? What happened?"

"Mom, you're in the ER and you're worried about me?" Sarah leaned over her mom and kissed her cheek, the smell of coconut lotion immediately making her homesick. "Just a little cut. I'm fine."

"I'm fine, too. I must have forgotten to eat and passed out."

A realization rolled over Sarah. "You can't go back home. You shouldn't be alone. You need help."

"I've never needed help." Her voice sounded

sleepy, confused. Yet determined. "I can take care of myself. You need to live your own life."

Loud voices sounded in the hall. Cold dread pooled in Sarah's gut even before she heard Nick practically shouting his greeting to "Officer Jimmy Braeden."

Sarah glanced around the room. A door to a small bathroom stood ajar. She pressed a kiss to her mother's cheek. "Mom, a friend of mine may be coming into the room. He's protecting me. His name's Nick Jennings." She glanced at the door, her heart jackhammering in her chest. "If he says you know his mother from church, go along with it." She rushed to get all the information out.

Her mother opened her eyes wide for the first time. "I'll never understand you, Sarah Lynn."

"Pretend you know him, Mom. And don't say anything about me being here."

Her mother lifted her hand slightly, then let it drop.

Through the glass of the door, she saw the back of Nick's head. She knew he was holding off Jimmy to give her time to hide. She ran to the bathroom and slid behind the door, pushing it almost closed, leaving a narrow view of the room through the crack. All she could see was a portion of her mother's face and the water jug on the side table.

The door to the room swooshed open. Nick's was the first voice she heard. "Hello, Mrs. Gardner. How are you?"

Her mother's gaze drifted to the bathroom. *No, Mom, don't look at me!*

"I've had better days."

Her mother lifted a hand to her hair, as if to fluff it up. Despite Sarah's racing heart and dry mouth, she couldn't help but smile. Her mother always flirted with the handsome men. And Nick was definitely handsome.

"This man claims you know his mother." The voice of Jimmy had Sarah closing her eyes. She tried to imagine herself invisible behind the bathroom door. Pinpricks of panic raced across her scalp.

"Of course I know his mother. From church." *Good, Mom.*

"I appreciate your looking out for me, Jimmy, but I'm very tired. I could use some rest."

"Of course. I'll check in on you tomorrow morning. Need anything?"

Sarah gathered the courage to peek, and her mother shook her head. "Jimmy, you don't need to fuss over me. I know you and my Sarah are no longer together. You don't owe me anything."

"You're no trouble at all, Mrs. Gardner. I like to keep tabs on those I care about." The tightness in his voice made Sarah's blood turn cold in her veins. "Whose baseball cap is this?"

Sarah sucked in a breath and pressed her back against the wall, wishing she could melt into it. How had she been so careless as to leave her cap?

"Baseball cap?" Her mother sounded confused.

"Yeah, same college as Sarah's."

Her mother didn't say anything.

"Have you seen Sarah recently, Mrs. Gardner? She'd want to know you're in the hospital. I could contact her for you?"

Her mother made a sound Sarah couldn't decipher. "I'm fine. I don't need anyone to make a fuss over me."

"I'd be happy to check in on you," Nick said. "My mother's already planning your menu for the week. I hope you like chicken noodle soup."

Sarah closed her eyes. If she didn't know Nick was lying, she would have believed every word he was saying.

"Sounds lovely." Her mother's voice grew weaker.

"We should be going," Nick said, his voice full of authority.

Sarah couldn't see Jimmy or Nick from her hiding place, but she sensed Nick was ushering

Jimmy out the door. She feared Jimmy wasn't going to take kindly to being forced out.

"Good night, Mrs. Gardner. Please know my mother sends her best."

"Thank you." Her mother stared straight ahead. "Good night, Jimmy."

After a few moments, her mother turned toward the bathroom where she was hiding. "They're gone."

Sarah slipped out of the bathroom, keeping her eye on the door to the hallway. Pressing her hand to her chest, she heaved a heavy sigh. "That was too close."

"I hate seeing you like this," her mother whispered, as if afraid to make the admission.

"I hate it, too, but Jimmy's dangerous." Sarah touched her throat, remembering the time Jimmy held her against the wall with one hand around her neck. She pressed charges the next day.

That's when Jimmy's smear campaign started in earnest. When the battle seemed insurmountable, she fled town.

Her mother gestured toward her. "Let me hold your hand."

Sarah gave her a shaky smile.

"There's something I haven't told you." There was a clarity in her mother's eyes she hadn't noticed before.

A cold, icy knot tightened in Sarah's belly. "There's nothing more the doctors can do."

For her cancer?

All the appropriate phrases slammed into Sarah's brain:

No, there has to be something.

Are you sure?

No, no, no!

But instead Sarah bent down and buried her nose in her mother's hair and cried. "I'm sorry."

Sarah pulled back so she could read her mother's expression. "I know. I know. Don't cry."

Sarah sniffed, trying to pull it together and forgetting for once to look over her shoulder for fear the man who threatened to kill her would make good on his promise.

Nick couldn't bear to listen to Sarah's quiet sobs in the passenger seat as they headed back to Apple Creek after visiting Mrs. Gardner. He hardly knew this woman sitting next to him, but his heart broke for both her and her mother.

After escorting Jimmy out of Mrs. Gardner's room, Nick had waited in the car near the ER entrance, ever vigilant that Jimmy could return at any moment. Nick didn't let down his guard until Sarah had returned to the car after saying goodbye to her mother.

They switched back to his truck at one of his

father's offices about forty-five minutes outside of Apple Creek. Nick's heartache for Sarah morphed into renewed anger against Jimmy. Why did some men feel the need to control women? Hot anger pulsed through his veins. Jimmy had already cost Sarah her job in Buffalo. Her home. Was Nick going to allow Jimmy to make her miss being with her mother in her time of need?

Nick glanced over to his passenger and noticed her head was dipping at an awkward angle. She was exhausted. "Sarah," he whispered. "Sarah?"

She didn't answer. He dug the phone out of his pocket and dialed his sister's number. He didn't want to use his Bluetooth connection for fear the voice booming over the speaker would wake Sarah.

His sister Christina answered after the second ring. "Hey there, sister."

"Something wrong?" she asked, worry lacing her tone.

"Why do you think something has to be wrong for me to call my baby sister?"

Nick could imagine her "give me more credit than that" look with her fisted hand planted on her narrow waist.

"It's late. I know. I'm sorry. Sarah's mom needs hospice care." Sarah told Nick the devastating news that the doctors had exhausted treatment options for her mother. He glanced over as they passed under a streetlight, and he caught a flicker of Sarah's peaceful face, even if her neck was cricked at an awkward angle.

"You want to know if I can provide care if you bring Mrs. Gardner to Apple Creek to live with Sarah."

"Whoever said you weren't smart..." He felt a smile pulling at his lips. Bringing Mrs. Gardner to Apple Creek would solve a lot of his concerns. Sarah could be with her mom, and Nick could protect Sarah.

"Who said I wasn't smart?" Christina said playfully, then she grew quiet. "That's too bad about her mom. How's Sarah taking it?"

"As well as can be expected."

"Does Sarah plan to stay in Apple Creek? And is her mom willing to come here?"

Nick turned toward the driver's side window and whispered in a low voice. "It's yet to be determined. But I wanted to explore all options before I make any suggestions."

A long silence stretched across the line. "Nick, this woman's important to you, isn't she?"

Nick didn't dare look to see if Sarah was awake. Mostly, he was glad she couldn't hear his sister's end of the conversation. "Yeah."

"She's right there, isn't she?"

"Yeah," he said, ever more cryptic. "Can you meet us at the house in ten minutes? Bring stuff to stay over? I don't think she should be alone."

"I'll do whatever I can to help you, Sarah and her mother. I love you, big brother."

"I love you, too." Nick ended the call and set the phone on the middle console.

"I'm sorry I'm not very good company," Sarah said in a sleepy voice.

"You must be exhausted."

"I am."

"You've had a rough—"

"Couple years."

Nick slowed and turned up the bumpy driveway to her rented cottage. He glanced up at the darkened home. Only a small light glowed from the Zooks' home next door. "I don't like you staying here all by yourself."

Sarah tipped her head back on the seat and sighed heavily. She pressed the heels of her hands into her eyes. "I'm too tired to think. Who were you talking to?"

"My sister."

"Hmm," Sarah said, still dreamily. "You guys are close."

"Yes, we are."

"I was an only child." There was a wistful

quality to her tone. "Did you tell her she had to stay at the house with me?"

"Listen, Sarah," Nick shifted in his seat to face her more fully. "I have an idea."

Sarah yawned. "Can we get out of the car and talk about it? I need to walk. Get some blood circulating before I fall asleep again."

"Sure." Nick climbed out of the truck and went around and opened Sarah's door. She squinted against the glow of the dome light. He couldn't help but notice that her eyes were red from the combination of tears and exhaustion.

"It's a nice night." Nick reached for her hand and helped her. Her hand felt cool and delicate in his. *What was it about this woman?* Was he drawn to her or the need to protect her?

Or both.

When they reached the steps, she pulled her hand out of his, as if just now realizing they were walking hand in hand. "What is it you wanted to talk about?"

"Why don't you bring your mother here?"

Sarah jerked her head back. "To Apple Creek?"

"Yes, my sister agreed to monitor your mother's health while she's here. Since…" He stopped himself, not wanting to remind her of what she'd likely never forget. Mrs. Gardner's condition was beyond treatment. Mostly likely, she'd be given medications for pain and maintenance.

"You've been too kind." She brushed a hand across his cheek. "But I don't think my mom would leave her house." She worked her lower lip. "I'm going to have to seriously consider leaving Apple Creek. My mom needs me back in Buffalo."

"Please, give my suggestion some thought." Nick wanted to be the one to protect Sarah. He couldn't do that if she moved an hour away. And especially not if she moved back near Jimmy. "Talk to your mom about it."

Sarah laughed. "You don't know my mom. She's pretty stubborn."

"Like mother like daughter."

Sarah rewarded him with a quiet laugh. "Then you should know better than to argue with me." She reached for the handle on the screen door. "Good night, Nick."

"Hold up. My sister is on the way over to stay with you."

Sarah's eyes widened. "Oh, I can't put her out."

"She doesn't mind." Nick brushed a tear from her cheek with the back of his fingers. "Besides, I'm sure she'll ask me for a really big favor down the road." He tried to lighten the mood. "That's what family is for, right?"

The sound of tires on gravel had him turn toward the road. He recognized his sister's sedan. "She's here. You wouldn't want her to have come all this way for nothing."

Nick reached out and squeezed Sarah's hand. "It's going to be okay."

"You really shouldn't have asked her..." Sarah stood with a hand on her hip and the other palm flattened against the propped open screen door. When she realized this was really happening, she finally agreed.

"Glad to hear reason has won out." Nick glanced over to his sister's car. She was talking on her phone. "Let me check the house, then I'll help my sister."

Nick checked the house, then went back outside.

Christina had climbed out of her car and was standing next to her open trunk. Nick crossed the yard, kissed his sister's cheek, then grabbed her duffel bag. "Thanks. I owe you."

"Of course you do," Christina said and playfully tapped him on the arm. Then she lowered her voice. "What did she think about bringing her mother here?"

"She's not convinced. She believes her mother will be more comfortable in her own home."

"We'll convince her mom," Christina said in the easy manner of someone who confidently dealt in life-and-death situations on a regular basis.

Once inside the house, Christina admired the space. "How cozy. I've been looking for a little place myself." His sister had been so busy trying to save the world, she hadn't really settled anywhere. Ever since she had returned to Apple Creek a few years ago, she had been renting one half of a duplex near Main Street. The only furnishings as far as he knew were the ones the landlord had provided.

"You could move into mother and father's house. I don't think they've been home from Europe since Christmas," Nick said.

"Do you really see me living in mom and dad's house? I need to be able to connect to my patients. Living there would send the wrong message."

Sarah stepped out of the small half bath patting her face with a pink hand towel. She forced a bright smile that didn't reach her sad eyes. "Nick shouldn't have called you. I hate to put you out. I'm fine here."

Christina touched Sarah's arm. "I'm sorry about your mom."

Sarah pressed her lips together and nodded. "Thanks." Her lips parted, as if she wanted to say more, but didn't.

"Well, it's been a long day," Nick said, "I'll let you get settled."

Sarah looked up and they locked gazes.

"Thank you. If it weren't for you, I wouldn't have been there for my mom today." Her voice broke over the word *today*.

Nick hooked his thumbs in his jeans pockets, not knowing how to comfort her. Not knowing what was appropriate. Christina pulled Sarah into an embrace. Something he wanted to do, but felt it wasn't his place.

His sister pulled away and held Sarah at arm's length. Sarah met his gaze and her cheeks turned pink. "I'm a mess. I'm sorry."

"No need to apologize." Nick shifted his stance.

"I suggest you take Nick and me up on our offer to help care for your mother here in Apple Creek," Christina said. "You'll both feel better being around one another."

"I'm afraid Jimmy already knows where I am."

"What if he doesn't? We should be careful anyway," Christina said. "I can work with you and the hospital to have your mom released to a sister in Florida."

Sarah's eyebrows arched. "My aunt does live in Florida."

"Well, we'll contact her to make sure she's in on the ruse in case your ex tries to verify this. He'll run into a dead end."

"Assuming Jimmy hasn't already found me."

Sarah kept coming back to this point. She pushed her bangs off her forehead. A beige bandage still covered her stitches. She looked like she wanted to argue, but she settled on a simple, "I don't think my mom will go for it."

"You won't know until you ask." Christina glanced around the room. "I'm sorry to hear the doctors no longer feel they can treat your mother's cancer. But I can help make the time she has left comfortable. You have enough room here if you need to bring a hospital bed in."

Sarah pressed a hand to her cheek and wrapped the other arm around her thin waist. She nodded in agreement.

Sarah pressed her trembling lips together as a silent tear slipped down her cheek. "Can we really do this?"

"There's no reason we can't."

Hope blossomed in Nick's heart. He felt a little selfish because this also meant Sarah wouldn't be going anywhere.

"Between the two of us, we can make sure your mom is well cared for."

Sarah bowed her head and dragged her wet cheek across her shoulder. "I...I..."

"Ask your mom. You owe her and *yourself* that much," Nick said.

"She can't be alone and I'm her only daughter." Her voice shook.

An unreadable expression flashed across Sarah's face. "But what about Jimmy or whoever is harassing me? I don't want my mom harassed during her…final days." She closed her eyes briefly. "Oh, but he'd harass us for sure in Buffalo." Her words dripped with the agony of her impossible situation.

"If your mom decides to move in here, I'll set up a cot in the back room near the door." The idea struck Nick two seconds before he suggested it. *Was he crazy?* "Just until we catch whoever is harassing you," he quickly added.

"Do you think it's Jimmy? Your friend said he was working Sunday night."

"Doesn't mean he didn't sneak down to Apple Creek. But, I don't know…seems a little too juvenile for a mean guy like Jimmy. I've known guys like him. Controlling. Just plain mean. I think if it were him, he wouldn't have stopped with a threat. He would have…" he let his words trail off, realizing he was frightening her. Sarah appeared to be trembling. Christina must have sensed it at the same time. She took Sarah's elbow and guided her to the couch.

"I'll get you some water." Christina hustled into the kitchen.

"Jimmy liked to toy with me. Going in for the kill right away wasn't sporting of him," Sarah said in a mocking voice.

"I'll keep you safe."

"How? You can't be with me all the time."

Nick's stomach dropped. She was right.

"I can try."

"Oh, I don't know..." Sarah had a wary look in her eyes. "What would that look like? You staying here?"

"Your mom can be your chaperone," Christina said cheerily as she returned with Sarah's water. "Until then, I'll stay with you."

"My mom loves her house. Her friends at church..."

"You could think of all the reasons why it wouldn't work, or you can just have a little faith." Nick slipped in and sat next to her.

Sarah nodded slowly.

"It's late. Why don't you get some sleep?" He pushed to his feet. He kissed his sister's cheek. "Thank you." Then he turned to face Sarah. "We'll go back to Buffalo in the morning and invite your mom to come home with you."

Sarah's brow creased. "Don't you have to work?"

"I have the day off."

"Oh, okay." She seemed hesitant, almost disappointed that she had run out of excuses. "But it won't be her home." Sarah's voice was racked with worry.

"I have a feeling your mom will consider home anywhere you are."

Sarah stood and touched his arm. "You're a good man, Nick. Thank you."

EIGHT

A few days after Christina's suggestion that Sarah's mom move to Apple Creek, she had. Now, Sarah's mother had been here almost a week and seemed to be settling in, and Christina graciously managed her care. Sarah tried not to think of the reality of her mother's situation and instead cherished each day.

Tears burned the back of Sarah's eyes. Wasn't this what faith was all about? Trusting in God's plan? Sarah collected the dishes from the kitchen table. She dumped the cereal from her mother's partially eaten breakfast down the disposal.

Nick kept watch every evening, usually arriving close to dark and leaving at dawn. Sarah guessed he didn't want to impose on her time with her mother.

Through the window above the sink, she watched Mary Ruth take Sarah's mother by the elbow and help guide her down the back steps.

Her mother had everyone, including Sarah, calling her Maggie, and Sarah was seeing a side to her mother that she never had. Her mother—*Maggie*—had interests that extended beyond being Sarah's mother. It shouldn't have surprised Sarah, but it did. The two of them had developed such a strong mother-daughter bond after her father died that it was hard to separate the person from that of her mother.

Maggie had taken to strolls around the property, surprising for a woman who rarely ventured out of her own home. Maybe it was because she was always too busy cooking, cleaning and otherwise tending to a house. Things she had struggled to do of late.

Other than the weight of her mother's illness, Sarah had been able to take somewhat of a breath. There hadn't been any other "incidents," and if Jimmy did know where she was, he probably would have sought her out once her mother disappeared.

Yet, all had been quiet.

Maybe Jimmy believed the false story they had planted that her mother moved to Florida with Sarah's aunt.

Maybe it had been the foolish youth trying to mess with her. She had another Sunday meeting in a few days. Two weeks from the original episode. She debated bringing it up for fear she'd push those away who needed her most.

Sarah put the last dish in the dishwasher and dried her hands on the towel hanging over the handle of the oven. She was growing fond of the quiet routine of the days since her mother had arrived. She had reluctantly rescheduled clients, but it needed to be done. She wished she could bottle this time.

Sarah slipped her feet into her shoes and ran across the yard to join Mary Ruth and her mother as they strolled the perimeter of the yard, one side bordered by Apple Creek, the body of water after which the town was named.

"Beautiful morning," Sarah said. Birds chirped and the wind rustled through the ever-growing corn.

"Mary Ruth has been sharing tidbits about the Amish life," her mother said, her words wrapped around little gasps for air. A condition that was sure to get worse.

"What have you learned?" Sarah smiled.

"Well, I'm amazed that the Amish don't go to school past eighth grade."

"Why would we need an education when most of us end up right here on the farm?" If Sarah hadn't been watching Mary Ruth's face, she might have missed the flicker of regret.

"Teenage *Englischers*—" Sarah used the

word the Amish would for people like herself "—would love to drop out of school." She had tried to lighten the tone, but it only made Mary Ruth more thoughtful.

"I guess people don't realize what they have."

Sarah's gaze drifted from her mother to Mary Ruth. "I've never heard you talk about school."

Mary Ruth shrugged, the straps of her bonnet dangling near her shoulders. "Ever since my brother hopped the fence and then I called things off with Ruben, I've been thinking..."

An uneasy feeling dimmed the edges of the glorious late-summer morning.

"I always wished I had gone to college," Maggie said. "But money was tight growing up. So, I went to work." She said it so matter-of-factly, as if she never had a choice and the path of her life had been predetermined.

It broke Sarah's heart how her mother spoke of her past in the way older people did when they were coming to the end of the road. Her mother, by rights, should have had many more years on earth. Many more years.

"I suppose we've all had regrets," Sarah said, stuffing the tips of her fingers into the back pockets of her jeans.

Her mother stopped and turned to face her. "Don't go feeling sorry for yourself since Jimmy turned out to be a no-good creep." Her mother grabbed Sarah's arm and gently shook her. "It's not your fault."

Sarah pressed her lips together, afraid to speak. Afraid her voice would tremble. Afraid she'd start crying and never stop. And she was tired of every conversation gravitating back to her. This was about Mary Ruth.

"Have you ever considered getting your GED?" Sarah asked. "It's the equivalent of a high school diploma."

"I'm not sure I'm book smart." A soft smile curved the corners of Mary Ruth's mouth. "Not like you."

Sarah shook her head. "Don't dismiss yourself."

"I'm not," Mary Ruth said assuredly, then she got a gleam in her eye. "I'm glad you came to Apple Creek. I'm sorry it was under these circumstances."

Impulsively, Sarah reached over and gave Mary Ruth a hug. The young Amish girl stiffened, then returned the embrace. Sarah was the first to pull away. "I didn't mean to make you uncomfortable."

Mary Ruth waved her hand. "The Amish aren't big on displays of affection."

Both Mary Ruth and Sarah turned when they heard her mother laugh. "Sarah was never the most affectionate person, either." She chuckled again, a delightful sound.

They reached a bench at the far corner of the yard where the Zooks' property ended at the creek. The water wound along the edge of a path bordering thick foliage. Nick had been kind enough to build the bench, specifically so Maggie could rest during her walks. Sarah's heart warmed at the simple kindness of this man. A man she had grown to learn was filled with much kindness and compassion, a far cry from her ex.

Her mother sat and ran her hands down the thighs of her jeans. "I feel rejuvenated here." She looked up with radiant eyes and reached for Sarah's hand and pulled her down next to her. "I'll never regret my coming to Apple Creek. I had held onto the house in Buffalo because it was my house with your father, but I can't turn back the hands of time. Your father's been gone a long time, and without you there, it didn't feel like home."

Sarah bowed her head, afraid to let her mother see the tears in her eyes. "You shouldn't have had to leave your home, especially not now."

"You shouldn't have had to leave your home, either. But you're doing well here in Apple Creek. Helping people. And I feel like I'm on a vacation. I don't have to look around the house and feel bad about all the things I can no longer do—gardening, cleaning, cooking. I'm enjoying my time here. All those chores left me feeling exhausted." Her voice cracked over the last words. Her mother lifted her hand and cupped Sarah's cheek. "We're blessed to have this time together. Never regret that."

Sarah lifted her eyes to meet her mother's gaze. They both had tears in their eyes. Sarah hugged her mom and held on tight, memorizing this moment. "I love you."

"I love you, too."

Sarah turned to see Mary Ruth had tears in her eyes, too. Sarah laughed. "Look at us, a sorry bunch."

Mary Ruth shrugged and glanced over her shoulder toward the barn next door. "Your mom said she'd like to see the horses."

Her mother nodded. "City girl that I am, I can count on one hand how many times I've come up close and personal with a horse."

"Really?" Mary Ruth said, not hiding the surprise from her voice.

"It must sound strange from someone who lives on the farm and uses them for transportation."

"It's funny. When I was younger, I used to watch cars go whizzing down the street and wonder where they were going. I'd daydream about the world outside. But that's not the Amish way," she quickly added.

"We all wonder about the what-ifs…" her mother's voice had a distant quality to it. "But—" Maggie's voice brightened "—I don't want my Sarah to ever wonder *what if* she had taken a chance on that handsome Deputy Jennings."

"Mom!" Sarah admonished playfully, suddenly envisioning Nick's warm brown eyes, his broad shoulders, his unshaven jaw. "He's just being nice." She tried to shake the image.

"You could use someone nice." Her mother grabbed the arm of the bench and pushed herself to a standing position. Sarah resisted the urge to jump up and help every time her mother did something. She knew her mother wouldn't want to be fussed over every second.

"Deputy Jennings *is* a very nice man. I've noticed him drive by quite often when he's working."

"He's doing his job, making sure I'm safe. I appreciate that he left his truck here in case we need transportation."

"You can make all the excuses you want, Sarah Lynn. But don't let your past dictate your future."

Sarah smiled, but didn't say anything.

"Can I see those horses?" her mother asked Mary Ruth.

"Sure. I saw little Patience playing by the barn. She'd be happy to show you her family's animals." It went without saying that Mary Ruth hoped she wouldn't run into Ruben.

"If you don't mind, I'm going to go in and do some paperwork."

Her mother waved her hand. "Go, go. We'll be fine."

Sarah watched her mother walk slowly next to Mary Ruth. She took comfort in knowing that her mother did seem content, despite her health and relocation.

Thank You, Lord.

Sometimes the simplest prayer was one of gratitude.

Thank You.

When Sarah reached the back door, she heard her cell phone ringing. Nick had insisted she have one. He had registered it in his name and only a few trusted people had her number. She ran up the steps and into the house and grabbed the phone off the kitchen counter. She didn't recognize the number.

"Hello?"

"Hello," came the quiet voice, "is this Sarah Lynn?" Not everyone knew her full name.

"Yes?"

"Hi, I got your name from the pastor at Apple Creek Community Church. He told me you might be able to help me…" The woman's voice trailed off, and Sarah thought she heard her sniffle.

"Is everything okay?"

"No, I'm afraid my baby and I can't afford food, and I'm worried."

"The church has a food pantry."

"I don't have a car, and I've reached my wit's end."

Sarah paced the kitchen, and as the woman explained her dire situation, Nick's truck parked in the driveway came to mind.

"What's your name?"

A long pause stretched over the line. "I'm Jade Johnston. I live on the old farm on Route 62 out past the Troyers' garden nursery."

"Do you have food for your baby for today?"

Sarah thought she heard a child cry in the background, but she couldn't be sure.

"I'm so stupid. I don't know how I got myself in this situation. The baby's always hungry."

"Is the baby still on formula?" Sarah's mind raced.

"No, no. The baby's two."

"Okay." Sarah thought about calling Nick,

but he was working and he had done so much for her already.

What could it hurt to help this woman? It would only take a few minutes, and she had the truck. She wouldn't be walking along the road, exposed.

"I'll bring some groceries to you today. And then we'll have to fill out some paperwork to make sure you and your baby have services until you get on your feet again."

"Oh, that would be great. Thank you."

Sarah ended the call, and something uneasy banded around her lungs. As she wrote a note to her mother and Mary Ruth and then climbed into Nick's truck, she assured herself her feelings of unease stemmed from the woman's desperate call and not her apprehension of driving out to an unfamiliar house alone.

Sarah turned the key in the ignition, dismissing her anxiety as one of the hazards of being a social worker. Always cautious.

Nick always looked forward to his lunch break at the Apple Creek Diner. He parked his cruiser along the curb and strolled inside. He tipped his hat at the couple sitting in the booth by the window. The elderly pair seemed to have claimed that table as their own.

Nick had grown up in Apple Creek. Despite

his parents' wealth, they had insisted on public education through high school. After he graduated, he joined the service. His parents, who understood the need to follow one's passion, didn't dissuade him from going into law enforcement, although they would have preferred a safer path.

Nick had been back in Apple Creek a year, and he was still trying to get accustomed to the fact that everyone seemed to think they knew him. When most of them only knew that he was one of the Jennings' kids who grew up in the big house on the escarpment. They didn't truly know him.

Anonymity didn't exist in small towns.

"Hello there, Nick." Flo the waitress strolled over to his table. *Point made.* "We have chocolate cream pie and lemon meringue today."

"Oh, tough choice. Let me have a BLT for now, and I'll give my dessert choice some careful consideration." A slow smile crept across his face.

Flo put in his order, then made her way back over to him. "I was surprised to see you pull up. I thought you might have had the day off or something."

Nick cocked his head in curiosity.

"I saw your truck go by not more than ten minutes ago. Thought maybe you were headed out for another picnic with that pretty social worker I've heard you've been spending time with."

Nick blinked slowly and laughed. Truly nothing got past the residents of Apple Creek.

"Shame about her mother. Curious that her mom would come to Apple Creek and Sarah didn't move back to Buffalo to help her while she's ill."

Apparently some rumors didn't get circulated. Namely, the one about Sarah being stalked by her ex-boyfriend. "I left her the truck in case she wanted to go somewhere with her mom."

Flo patted his shoulder. "You really are a good guy—" she leaned in conspiratorially "—despite what some people say."

Nick shook his head. "I can only imagine what *some* people say."

"I think it's a good thing you're doing. Helping her. Before you came along she seemed lost."

The cook dinged the bell. Flo strolled over to get his sandwich and returned, sliding the plate in front of him. "Have you decided on the pie?"

Nick twisted his lips, as if it were a hardship to decide. "I'm feeling chocolate cream today."

"Sounds good. I'll bring you a slice after you finish your sandwich."

The bells on the door chimed, and Flo walked

away to seat a couple young men who were most likely taking summer classes on the nearby campus.

Alone with his sandwich and his thoughts, Nick couldn't help but wonder where Sarah was headed in his truck. She had seemed reluctant for him to leave it there, but he had insisted. He didn't like the idea of her isolated with a sick mother and a potential stalker around. Even though that hadn't been his intent, Sarah had told him she'd only use it in a true emergency.

Nick's heart sank. *Had something happened?*

Nick grabbed his cell phone from his utility belt and stared at it a minute before dialing. He didn't want Sarah to feel uncomfortable about using his truck—even if it was to do a grocery run—but a little voice in the back of his head nudged him to check in with her. To make sure she and her mother were okay. Sure, everything had been quiet recently, but that didn't mean Jimmy wasn't lying in wait.

The thought sent renewed anger pulsing through his veins. He put down his sandwich and dialed Sarah's number. He held his breath, waiting for her to answer.

She answered, sounding like she had run to the phone.

"Where are you?"

Sarah gave her location before she paused midsentence and let out a bloodcurdling scream.

"Sarah! Sarah!" he yelled into the phone, but his pleas were only met with silence.

NINE

Sarah slowed the truck as it climbed the crest on Route 62. She'd passed the Troyers' nursery about a half mile back and knew the farm where the woman called from for assistance had to be just ahead. Sarah wasn't used to driving such a big vehicle and worried if she'd be able to navigate it up the driveway over a small wooden bridge over a ditch lining the country road. Many a drunk driver had ended up in a ditch along country roads in the dark of night.

Why did most of her nervousness surrounding driving always have to circle around to her dad's tragic accident? *Accident?* The man that had chosen to drink and then drive had killed her dad. That was no accident. He had acted willingly. Foolishly. Recklessly.

Sarah shoved the thought aside and focused instead on this good deed. This was how she had gotten through life. Refocus all her negative energy on good deeds. Helping others.

Her mother was right about her need to become a social worker. *Worker, heal thyself.*

If only.

She turned up the driveway and gripped the steering wheel tightly as the weight of the truck made the wooden slats of the makeshift bridge over the ditch groan. Calling to tell Nick he could retrieve his truck from a trench wasn't on her list of things she wanted to do. He had already gone too far out of his way for her.

Not to mention her strong desire *not* to be stranded in the middle of nowhere. She glanced over at her purse on the passenger seat, grateful she had a phone.

Sarah parked the truck alongside a broken-down home with gray siding that probably hadn't seen the underside of a paintbrush in fifty years. An abandoned Amish buggy sat unused and broken next to a barn farther back on the property. She had automatically assumed the caller was not Amish and figured that still might be the case, considering it wasn't unusual for the Amish to sell their homes to the *Englisch* and vice versa. She squinted through the windshield. Someone lived here? A child, no less?

Unease and goose bumps swept across her skin. Maybe it hadn't been a good idea to venture out here alone.

Before she lost her nerve, Sarah pushed open

the truck's door and stepped out. Renewed determination to help this small family urged her forward. If she didn't help them, it was likely no one would.

Sarah grabbed the two bags of groceries she had picked up at the store, not wanting to take the time to visit the food pantry at church. God forgive her, but there was no such thing as a quick visit to the church with the pastor's wife there. She was a talker.

Sarah grabbed the handles of the plastic bags and strode toward the door. Dappled light filtered through the branches onto the pathway, stepping stones littered with brown pine needles. The word *isolated* popped into her mind. She pushed her shoulders back, much as she had done when approaching a new client's house, especially in a tough neighborhood.

Never let them see you sweat.

Sarah knocked on the door, and much to her surprise, it swung open on creaky hinges.

"Hello?" She poked her head in. The room was sparse with garbage gathered in the corners. A stroller parked in the middle of the room was the only indication someone with a child lived here.

"Hello?" Pulse pounding in her ears, Sarah stepped into the room. A baby blanket was bunched up in the stroller with a stuffed animal. A bottle was abandoned in the pile. Sarah picked it up and sniffed it. The milk wasn't spoiled, so someone had been here recently with a baby.

Her heart sank when she thought of a baby living in this squalor. A stale, dusty scent tickled her nose.

"Hello," she called again, her voice squeaky. All her training taught her to wait outside, make herself aware of her surroundings. Yet here she was standing in the middle of a seemingly deserted house.

All alone.

A breeze lifted the torn lacy curtain covering the window, and a shiver raced down Sarah's spine.

Sarah spun around and ran out of the house the way she had come in, suddenly feeling vulnerable. When she stepped outside, a breeze whispered across her damp skin.

Her ears perked when she heard a dog barking around back. Relief washed over her. *They must have stepped outside and didn't hear me at the front door.*

Adjusting the grocery bags in her grip, she made her way to the back, watching her step on the uneven ground. When she reached the other side of the house, abandoned toys from a yellow dump truck to a red plastic wagon littered the yard. On closer inspection, it seemed someone had used the neglected Amish buggy as a climbing toy. A child had left a small car on the seat.

Sarah set the groceries on a shaded patch under a large tree in the yard. Rubbing her palms together, she spun around to listen for the dog again. Maybe it had been a neighbor's pet.

Then she heard it. The barking sounded like it was coming from inside the barn. The barn—in a state of disrepair much like the house—sat in a strip of sun, making it seem less ominous. The barking grew frantic now, and Sarah wondered what was wrong. Perhaps the young woman who had called her had been hurt.

What about her baby?

Breaking into a jog, Sarah reached the open barn door. It took her eyes a minute to adjust to the heavy shadows broken up by sunlight slipping in through wooden slats, shrunken over time. The barking seemed to be coming from above her. That's when she saw him. A fluffy white dog standing on the ledge of the loft barking at her.

Sarah glanced around. Other than a few rusted tools, the barn, like the house, seemed to be uninhabited.

"How'd you get up there?" she said to the dog while approaching the loft. A ladder rested against the edge, and her confused mind wondered if the dog had climbed the ladder.

That wasn't possible, was it?

Sarah knew she couldn't leave the dog up there. If no one came for it, he'd die of thirst.

But how did he get up there?

Sarah grabbed her phone out of her purse and stuffed it into the back pocket of her jeans, feeling better about having it with her. She put her purse down on the straw-covered ground and grabbed a rung of the ladder. She shook it, trying to determine if it would hold her weight. It seemed pretty solid, and she didn't weigh that much.

The dog barked frantically down at her. The urge to rescue the dog and get back home was suddenly overwhelming.

Cautiously, she climbed the first few rungs of the ladder. The third rung creaked under her weight. Afraid she'd lose her nerve, she rushed to the top. When she reached the edge of the loft, the furry dog licked her face. "Hold on." Sarah scrunched up her face against the onslaught of kisses. "Back up so I don't fall." She laughed at the dog's enthusiasm. "How did you get up here anyway?" She grabbed on to the top of the ladder with one hand and held the dog back with the other. She debated for a minute how she was going to tuck the dog under her arm and navigate the ladder.

Holding on tight, she glanced down at the ground. From up here, it seemed much farther than when she was at the bottom looking up. Her knees grew weak.

This was so not a good idea. Didn't fire departments rescue animals? The phone she had stuffed into the back pocket of her jeans rang. She grabbed it with the hand that she had been holding the dog's collar with, and the furry animal took the opportunity to lick her squarely on the cheek. "Cut it out," she said before answering the call.

"Hello."

"Hey, where are you?"

"I'm at a farm on Route 62 just past the Troyers' nursery. I got a call from…" Out of the corner of her eye she saw a shadow explode out of the dark corner and bear down on her. A scream ripped from her throat as she dropped the cell phone.

She watched it smash against the barn floor in disbelief.

Panic had her scrambling down the ladder before she lost her balance and tumbled to the ground.

And then nothing.

* * *

Nick tossed money on the table, more than enough to cover his meal and tip, even though the diner offered those in law enforcement a meal for free. He jogged out to his patrol vehicle and flipped on the lights and headed toward Route 62 and the Troyers' nursery.

Strangely, he found himself saying a quick prayer for Sarah's safety. He hadn't said a prayer since he had been in a war-torn country, where the constant battles, death and destruction wore on him, making him question why he even bothered.

Just past the nursery, he slowed and glanced at each farm as he passed by. There weren't too many, but then he saw his truck parked in front of an old house and he couldn't help but mutter, "Thank You, Lord."

His relief was short lived when he noticed the windshield of his truck was smashed. Nick glanced around, but didn't see any sign of Sarah.

"Sarah!" he called.

No answer.

He jogged up to the house and found the front door ajar. "Sheriff's deputy," he announced as he strode into the abandoned house. It appeared as if a squatter lived here. Yet, a relatively new-looking stroller sat in the middle of the room.

Had Sarah come here to help a young mother?

Where are you, Sarah?

Nick made his way out the back door where he heard a dog barking from the rundown barn. With his hand hovering over his weapon, he moved quickly to the barn. He flattened himself against the exterior barn wall and leaned around to peer into the barn, not wanting to make himself a target.

It took his eyes a minute to adjust to the heavy shadows. His attention was drawn to the loft, where a dog was barking frantically. Then his gaze dropped. Sarah lay on the ground, unconscious.

Nick quickly scanned the barn, and except for the barking dog and the back of the loft where he couldn't see, the place seemed deserted.

He crouched by Sarah's side and brushed her hair out of her face. A steady pulse beat in her throat, and once again he thought, *Thank You, Lord.*

"Sarah, Sarah… It's Nick. Wake up."

Sarah's face scrunched up, and then she opened her eyes and winced. "Oh…what happened?"

She tried to push up on an elbow, and Nick told her to relax. Stay put.

"I was hoping you could tell me what happened."

"I was called out here by a young mom who

needed assistance. When she wasn't home—" Sarah seemed to be struggling to piece together her memory of events "—I heard the dog." Her gaze drifted to the loft. "He's still up there. Someone else was up there." Her pale face grew whiter. "I was trying to get away and fell."

"Who? Did you see his face?"

She winced. "No."

"Stay put."

He aimed his gun toward the loft as he climbed the ladder slowly, hoping not to make a sound. To gain the advantage. Otherwise he was going to be in some serious trouble if someone appeared in the loft pointing a gun down at him.

The dog's barking grew frantic. *That* wasn't going to help him.

When Nick reached the top, he stared into the far reaches of the loft. The heavy shadows made it hard to discern if someone was lurking there. When nothing moved, he pulled himself onto the loft and tested his weight on the aged beams. Trusting that it was going to hold him, he moved swiftly to check each corner of the loft.

Empty.

Whoever had been waiting for Sarah was gone.

His stomach dropped. Sarah was alone on the

floor of the barn. He moved to the edge of the loft and breathed a sigh of relief when he saw Sarah sitting against a support beam.

"I thought I told you to stay put."

She lifted her palms. "I did. I think I sprained my ankle. I hope it's not broken." Thankfully, she had made it half way down the ladder before she fell.

Nick scooped up the dog under his arm and backed down the ladder. He put the fur ball down on the ground, and the dog promptly ran to Sarah and licked her.

A beautiful smile graced her face as she playfully tried to fend the rambunctious dog off. "Friendly little thing." She felt around his furry neck. "No collar."

"I want to get you to the health-care clinic. Check you out." Nick crouched next to Sarah and plucked a strand of hay out of her hair.

Her smile grew serious. "Jimmy's not going to stop, is he?"

"We don't know that it's him." Nick knew he was grasping at straws. They had to find a way to trap this guy.

"Who else would do this?" Sarah glanced up at the loft. "He wants to hurt me. He's mad that I left, and now he's toying with me. Making me suffer."

"Who called you out here?"

"A young woman. She said her name was Jade Johnston." She frowned and rubbed her forehead.

"We'll have to find her. Get her to answer some questions. But that can wait. Can you stand?" Nick asked, eager to get her safely home.

"On one foot." She scooted forward, and Nick wrapped his arm around her waist and pulled her up. Her hair smelled of flowers and hay, and a warmness surrounded his heart.

If only they had met under different circumstances. She wasn't in a relationship frame of mind, and he had been burned himself. But that wasn't something to think about now.

The dog barked at their feet.

Nick supported Sarah, and she tried to hop walk. She groaned as she leaned heavily on him. Suddenly, Nick had an urge to get out of here, fast.

"I'm going to carry you."

Before she had a chance to protest, he swept her off her feet. In an effort to lighten the mood, he grumbled, pretending she was heavy.

She playfully tapped his chest. "Thanks a lot." She pointed back to the fluffy little white dog. "We can't leave him here."

"Come on, girl," Nick said and the dog ran at his heels while he strode out of the barn, determined to tuck Sarah safely in his vehicle and get her away from this deserted place.

Immediately.

Sarah wrapped her arm around Nick's neck and tried to support her own weight. But each time she put weight on her one ankle, pain shot up her leg.

She appreciated his help, but she felt more than a little foolish when Nick lifted her, as if he were carrying a bride on her wedding day. With her aching ankle, she didn't have much choice. She just prayed it wasn't broken.

She was embarrassed that she had come out here alone and allowed herself to be a target.

Sarah hadn't exactly had a good year.

As Nick rounded the dilapidated house carrying her, Sarah's mind immediately went to the stroller she had found inside. But all thoughts of that disappeared when she saw his truck.

"Oh, your truck." The windshield was smashed. She felt sick to her stomach. "That's something Jimmy would do," she whispered. "He probably thinks we're dating, and he wants to destroy your truck." If he was watching her house he would have seen it parked there. He might have gotten the wrong idea.

Nick didn't slow his pace. When he reached his patrol vehicle, he put her down. Sarah supported herself on one foot on the hard-packed dirt. "I'm sorry."

"Lean against the car."

She did as she was told, and he unlocked the front passenger door and held it open for her. "Get in."

Nick helped guide her inside, then leaned across her to buckle her in. He smelled clean, like soap and aloe. She hated that she was causing so many problems for this sweet man.

He opened the back door for the dog and she hopped right in. "I'll swing back later and see if I can locate the owners."

Once he climbed in his side, he said, "Don't worry about my truck. That can be fixed."

Sarah tried to move her ankle and groaned. "I'm sure my ankle can be fixed, too."

Nick shifted in the driver's seat to face her. "We have to catch this guy. You shouldn't have to live like this, always looking over your shoulder."

Sarah's heart sank. "Maybe it's time for me to move."

A shadow crossed the depths of his eyes, eliciting an emotion she couldn't quite name. "Do you think running will solve your problems?"

Tears burned the back of her eyes. "Mom's sick. I can't subject her to this."

"And moving will be a good thing?"

"Of course not." Guilt and fear were her steady companions.

"You're safer in Apple Creek with me to protect you." As long as she stayed home.

Renewed anger boiled in her gut. She wasn't a violent person, but the way she felt right now, she could wring Jimmy's neck.

Without waiting for her reply, Nick started the car and turned around to get out of the driveway. "I'll have a tow truck pick up my truck later. We need to get you checked out at the clinic."

Sarah shifted in her seat, trying to get comfortable.

"I don't know what I'd do if I hadn't met you."

Sometimes God puts people in your path when you need them most.

Nick gave her a quick, sideways glance. "I'm glad you didn't have to find out."

TEN

The next few days were quiet as Sarah recuperated from her sprained ankle. Thankfully, it was just a sprained ankle. Her mother and she had caught up with a few episodes of their favorite show on Netflix. Their dog, who they named Lola, seemed content, like she had belonged to them all her life. Nick had tried to find her owner without success. Sarah was happy for the little fur ball.

Nick spent nights at her home, hoping to catch Jimmy—or whoever it was—in the act of harassing her, but mostly Sarah supposed Nick only caught a crick in his neck and bags under his eyes.

Nick still slipped in after dark and left just after the sun rose. It seemed he wanted to protect her, but not intrude on her life.

The phone number of the young woman who had called to lure Sarah to the abandoned barn had been a dead end. And according to county records, the house had been abandoned for three years. Jade Johnston didn't exist. Someone had been very careful.

"Hello," Mary Ruth called from the back door. "I brought dinner."

Sarah aimed the remote at the TV, and the screen went dark. She tried to respect Mary Ruth by keeping TV and other worldly things at a minimum when she was around. And lately, she had been a huge help, providing meals and companionship as Sarah recovered from a concussion and a sprain.

Sarah's mother was the first to get up from the couch. "Oh, Mary Ruth, you shouldn't have." Her mother lifted the lid on the dish and drew in a deep breath. "But we're so glad you did." Her mother set the dish on the table and grabbed three plates from the cabinet.

Leaning heavily on the arm of the couch, Sarah stood and carefully checked her weight on the sprain. It was definitely getting better. A tiny headache pulsed behind her eyes. Christina had said that was to be expected with a concussion. Sarah was also supposed to limit screen time, but staring at a blank wall was driving her crazy. When the TV started to bother her, she'd shut her eyes.

Mary Ruth strolled back to the door as if to leave.

"You have to join us," Sarah's mother said. "We enjoy your company."

Mary Ruth lifted her hand. "I really shouldn't."

"Do you have plans?" Sarah grabbed a few forks out of the drawer.

"No, but…"

"No, but nothing. Join us. My mother and I love your company."

Mary Ruth's face lit up. "I enjoy spending time with you, too." Then her voice grew soft. "I've been arguing a lot with my parents lately. It's easier for me to stay away because when I'm home, they're pestering me about talking to the bishop about baptismal classes." She tugged at her bonnet strings. "They question my choice in friends." Mary Ruth met Sarah's gaze.

Sarah's heart sank. "I wish they didn't feel that way. But I understand. Please let them know I respect your Amish ways and would do nothing to offend you."

Mary Ruth waved her hand and laughed. "Sometimes they think the Amish can do no wrong. But you and I know better." Sarah and Mary Ruth locked eyes. They had heard a lot at the group meetings from some of the Amish youth. Many things that would make the bishop question if they'd ever be ready for baptismal classes.

"All people make mistakes. All people deserve the opportunity to turn their lives around." Something niggled at the back of Sarah's brain. "In order to help people, we have to make sure what they tell us is kept in confidence."

Mary Ruth's face flushed bright red against her white bonnet. "I would never gossip about what goes on at the meetings at the church."

"I know you wouldn't." Sarah softened her tone. "But sometimes we don't think much of telling one person, who then tells another." She shrugged. "You know how it goes."

Mary Ruth got a worried look in her eyes that made Sarah uneasy.

"Is everything okay?" Sarah asked, feeling the tips of her fingers tingle.

"*Yah*, fine." Mary Ruth opened the cabinet and got out glasses. She had spent a lot of time here lately. "I worry that my parents will forbid me to continue helping you."

"What do you want to do, honey?" Maggie asked.

"I enjoy helping Sarah. Some of the Amish might not come to the meetings if I wasn't there. They'd be intimidated, or maybe think they were doing something wrong."

"Try to talk to your parents, and ultimately, you're an adult. Do what you feel is right," Sarah said, knowing that wasn't being truly fair. The Amish weren't brought up to do what they felt was right for themselves. They were taught to live with the community in mind.

With the final dinner preparations complete, they gathered around the table and said a silent prayer. Sarah took a bite of mashed potatoes and smiled. "I don't know what you put in these potatoes, but they're wonderful."

"They sure are," her mother said. "It makes me miss cooking." Her mother made a thoughtful expression, which meant she was up to something.

"What is it, Mom?"

"Wouldn't it be nice to host a picnic? I'd love to have corn on the cob, grilled chicken, fresh salad."

"You need to rest, Mom."

Her mother waved her hand in dismissal. "I feel great. I don't know if it's the country air or just knowing I don't have the burden of taking care of my home. I have the energy. I want to do this. Now, while I can. It would be a nice way to thank Mary Ruth and our neighbors for all their thoughtfulness while you've been laid up."

Sarah slowly flexed her ankle, testing to see if it still hurt. She had been a good patient and had been resting it. "I can help."

"I don't need help." Her mother smiled, transforming her face. "Let's do this."

Maggie's enthusiasm was contagious. As a social worker, Sarah knew that having a goal and something to look forward to often helped patients to maintain a positive outlook. A sense of shared enthusiasm had her grinning. "Okay, let's do this."

Her mother leaned over and planted a kiss on Sarah's forehead. "I'm so excited." She beamed, and Sarah tried to memorize the moment.

"Now, tell me, where can I find pen and paper? I want to make a list."

Sarah patted her mother's hand. "First, eat."

Mary Ruth lifted her glass in a quasi toast. "I can help with the picnic, too."

Nick came to the house earlier than usual that night, and he and Sarah went out onto the porch to talk.

"I'm not sure this picnic is such a good idea," Nick said, watching the sun dip low over the horizon. At times like this, he understood why his parents left the city and moved to the country. Nature could be spectacular.

Sarah leaned her head back on the rocking chair and sighed heavily. "My mom's excited. I don't want to take this away from her."

"We don't know what Jimmy's up to or if he's paid someone to harass you." Nick had contacted his friend who was doing him a favor by keeping tabs on Jimmy, and he reported back that Jimmy hadn't left the Buffalo area. The obvious answer was that Jimmy had paid someone to harass Sarah. Or, even more perplexing, someone altogether different had it out for her. Neither Sarah nor Nick wanted to believe their Amish friends would go to such lengths to hurt her.

Sarah leaned forward and glanced back at the house. Lowering her voice, she said, "I'm not going to let Jimmy take every little bit of joy out of our lives. My mother's time is limited. We're not going to stay locked up in the house for fear that Jimmy might or might not show up."

Nick ran his hands back and forth across the arms of the wooden rocker. She had a point.

"You'll be there, right?" Sarah angled her head up at him and smiled. "You'll protect us." The way she said the words—half serious, half dreamy—warmed his heart.

Nick couldn't help but smile at her eager face. He reached out and ran the back of his knuckle across her soft cheek. Her face flushed a soft pink. He pulled his hand away. "I'm sorry."

Sarah surprised him and reached out and touched his hand. "I'm not." She lifted her hand and touched his face. She grew serious.

Nick's heart raced, and he leaned forward and

brushed a kiss across her soft lips. He pulled away and studied her face. She blinked slowly, then a small smile graced her lips. He immediately wanted to kiss her again, but used restraint.

"So," she said playfully, "does this mean we're going to have a picnic?"

He raised an eyebrow. How could he say no to Sarah?

The day of the picnic was one of those glorious days in Western New York that made up for the months and months of winter with its cold temperatures and gigantic parking-lot snow piles. The sunshine and low humidity made living in this part of the country totally worth it.

Sarah stood in the doorway, holding a casserole dish she had just taken out of the oven. They couldn't have asked for a better day weatherwise. Her mother sat, head tipped in conversation with Miss Ellinor and Pastor Mike, on the wicker set they had moved from the front porch onto a patch of shaded lawn in the back. Maggie had a purple bandanna wrapped around her head. Her hair was slowly growing back now that she had stopped doing chemo.

Don't think about cancer today. Today is a celebration of summer. Of life.

The hiss of meat hitting the hot grill snapped her attention toward Nick, who stood at the fire with a fork in his hand. He looked comfortable at his station, as if he belonged there. At this house. With her. Neither had discussed their second kiss over a week ago, and it seemed like he was trying to avoid her. His last girlfriend must have really done a number on him.

Yet, he still came to her home late at night and left early in the morning, spending the night on the lumpy cot in the small room off the kitchen.

Her protector.

A warm breeze kicked up and blew a strand of hair across Sarah's face and tickled her nose. She didn't have a free hand to tug it away.

"Here, let me get that for you." Nick had put aside his grilling fork and took the casserole dish from her. Their fingers brushed in the exchange, and the memory of their kiss made her skin flush.

"Thank you."

Nick placed the dish on the table with the rest of the food. "The chicken's almost done."

"Great," Sarah said, suddenly not sure what to do with herself.

"Hey, I'm starving," Maggie called from across the yard. "What are you slowpokes doing?"

Sarah's heart filled with joy. Her mother really seemed to be doing well today. On days like this, she really missed her father. He should have been allowed to grow old and been there for his family.

Nick took the chicken off the grill and set it on the table, buffet style. The brothers, Ruben and Ephram, had lugged the long table from their barn. The Amish were well practiced at hosting a lot of people for meals. Every other week, one Amish family hosted the Sunday service and a meal afterward.

Christina and Mary Ruth strolled over to the table and sat down. The Zook family, minus their father, Amos, who was away at an auction, played a powder-puff game of volleyball. Temperance and Ephram against the younger siblings, Ruben and Patience. Mostly it seemed to be about letting Patience win. Sarah smiled, realizing some things were universal regardless of the cultural differences.

Sarah hoped that maybe Ruben and Mary Ruth could learn to be cordial, friends even. It was a small town, yet she hadn't noticed them talking. It was more a game of sticking to opposite sides of the yard.

"Does anyone need a fresh drink before we sit to eat?" Nick called. Before Sarah had a chance to take over, Nick walked away to collect the orders. Christina looked up at Sarah from the other side of the table. "I've never seen my brother look so happy."

Sarah tried to keep from smiling like the fool she was and sat down on the bench across from Nick's sister. "I was thinking the same thing about my mother." Instinctively, she changed the subject, uncertain of how to respond to what Christina had said. It didn't seem right that she could possibly make a man like Nick happy. He could have had any woman and certainly someone with far less baggage than she carried around.

"Your mother does seem happy." Christina lowered her voice and cut her gaze toward Maggie, who was still happily entertaining the pastor and his wife. Lola sat at her feet and enjoyed pats on the head from all of their guests. "Please don't hesitate to contact me if she gets uncomfortable. We can adjust her meds. There's a lot that can be done to make sure she remains pain-free."

Sarah nodded, unable to find the words. Every time she thought of her mother's illness taking over her body, a hollowness expanded inside her chest and crushed her lungs.

"I'm sorry, I shouldn't have brought that up right now." Christina reached between the tray of chicken and Miss Ellinor's famous potato salad and took Sarah's hand. "And don't think

I didn't notice how you deflected the topic of my brother."

Sarah furrowed her brow in mock confusion.

"My brother really likes you. Don't do anything to hurt him, okay?" Christina's breezy tone held a hint of warning.

A knot twisted in Sarah's stomach. "I would never do that. Not intentionally. But you know my situation. I may have to leave Apple Creek." And Nick.

"My brother would never tell you this, but his last girlfriend broke his heart. *Really* broke his heart." Sarah knew more than she should have thanks to Miss Ellinor.

Sarah tracked Nick as he walked across the yard, stopping to talk to her mother. He seemed at ease and comfortable in jeans and a golf shirt. *Man, he is handsome.*

"I have a hard time believing someone would do that to a guy like Nick." Sarah's gaze snapped to Christina's, and heat flooded her face, wondering why she kept talking.

"He has a good heart. Sometimes I think women want the bad boy. Outwardly, he may look like a bad boy, but he's not." She shrugged. "Amber broke up with him when he was overseas. Talk about low. Before he left, he had told me he could see being with her long-term." Christina pulled her hand away and brushed her bangs out of her eyes. "Anyway, I probably shouldn't tell you all his business. It's his story to tell. But he's my big brother and I love him and I see how he looks at you…"

Sarah ran her hand across the back of her neck, suddenly aware of every inch of her skin. Before she had a chance to say anything, Nick strolled over to them and handed each of them a soda. His gaze slid from his sister and then to Sarah. "What? Did I interrupt something?"

"Um…" Sarah let the word trail off.

Christina spoke up. "Sarah was saying how nice it was to have a man cook dinner for her."

Nick crossed his arms over his broad chest. "I wasn't cooking. I was manning the grill."

Sarah hitched an eyebrow. "Either way, the chicken looks great."

Nick's focus drifted to his sister. "I thought maybe you'd bring a date. Isn't it about time?"

Christina had been in the middle of taking a long swig of her soda, and she nearly spitted it out. "Way to get right to the point, big brother." Sarah had never seen the confident doctor blush before.

"Can't let one bad relationship stop you from finding another," Nick said, watching his sister carefully.

"Nice to know you take your own advice."

Christina gave her big brother a wicked grin, then turned to wink at Sarah.

"See, this is what she does. When she doesn't want to discuss her lack of social life, she turns it around on me." Nick playfully tugged a loose strand of his sister's hair.

"You asked for it."

Sarah smiled at the exchange. Growing up an only child had some advantages, such as having the sole attention of her parents, but she never enjoyed the camaraderie of a sibling. A sibling would be a wonderful asset right now as she dealt with her mother's health crisis.

Dread whispered across her brain. *When Mom dies, I'll be all alone.*

Just as Sarah's thoughts were traveling down a dark path, she noticed Patience tearing across the grass toward her home, her long dress flapping around her legs. "*Dat*'s home. *Dat*'s home!" Across the field, Amos climbed out of his wagon, and he seemed to be looking—glowering actually—in her direction.

Sarah stood and called to Ruben, who was still standing near the volleyball net. "Invite your father over. There's plenty of food."

All the color seemed to drain from Temperance's face. "It wonders me if it's not time we went home. Amos must be tired from his day, and he'll be looking for a quiet meal."

Maggie's face fell. "Oh, don't run off. We have all this food."

"I'm afraid we must." Something in Temperance's tone and rushed movements unnerved Sarah.

"Is everything okay?" Sarah asked, her attention shifting back to Amos, who worked with jerky movements to unhitch their horse from the wagon.

Temperance studied the ground for a moment before looking up. "Amos isn't very social. He likes to eat at home."

"That's a shame," Maggie said, her tone resigned.

Sarah smiled at her mother, feeling her disappointment. But Sarah also understood Temperance. She and Amos had a traditional Amish relationship where the wife deferred to the husband. Of course, every Amish relationship wasn't the same, but theirs was very traditional.

"May the children stay and eat?" Maggie asked, hope radiating from her bright eyes.

Temperance bit her lower lip. Ephram stepped forward and tipped his straw hat. "Thank you for your hospitality, but I'm afraid we should go."

Sarah felt Nick's hand on the small of her back and did her best not to lean into him. As much as she wanted to.

Sarah's gaze drifted to Mary Ruth, who sat quietly eating with a blank expression on her face. It was a shame Mary Ruth and Ruben didn't have much time to reconcile, even if only for friendship's sake.

The glorious afternoon had definitely shifted in mood.

"Who's going to have some of my potato salad?" Miss Ellinor walked over to the table and grabbed a sturdy disposable plate. God love Miss Ellinor.

"You know I'll have some." Pastor Mike accepted the plate his wife offered him.

Sarah looked up at Nick and fought back the tears. Her mother had been so excited about hosting a big picnic, and here it was falling apart.

A soft breeze picked up and the tiny hairs on her arms prickled to life. A horrible sense of foreboding weighed on Sarah's heart. A foreboding that seemed far too unreasonable for a picnic cut short.

ELEVEN

Nick carried a tray of dishes into the house and set them down on the counter next to the sink.

"Thanks." Sarah grabbed a dish and submerged it in the soapy water.

The sounds of a sitcom floated in from the other room. Nick poked his head in to see Maggie on the couch with her feet up on an ottoman. "Great picnic, Maggie."

She gave him a tired smile. "It was too bad the Zooks had to leave so soon, but I had a wonderful time all the same. Your sister is such a lovely girl. I'm blessed that a doctor of her caliber is right here in Apple Creek. She takes good care of me."

Nick smiled. "Christina is very good at her job, and you are a wonderful patient."

Maggie's cheeks colored. He had noticed a change in her since her first day in Apple Creek. She seemed relaxed. At peace. Nick tipped his head toward the kitchen. "I'm going to grab a few more trays from the yard."

Maggie shifted in her seat, as if to get up, when Nick waved his hand. "There's only a few things. I've got it."

Maggie smiled and sank back into the couch. "If you insist."

Sarah glanced over her shoulder at Nick. She lowered her voice. "This was a great day for my mom. She needed something like this." She turned on the water and rinsed the suds from the glass and placed it upside down in the drying rack. "It's too bad our neighbors couldn't stay. I haven't been able to shake this horrible feeling since they left. I'm not sure why."

"You wanted everything perfect for your mom. But she seems content. The picnic was, by all accounts, a success."

"Miss Ellinor is lively conversation. And your sister seemed to connect with Mary Ruth." She shook her head as if deep in thought. "I worry about Mary Ruth. She's at a fork in the road. Sometimes I worry—despite my best attempts—that I'm a negative influence."

Nick jerked his chin back. "I can't imagine."

"I worry that she longs to live a different kind of life. One with TVs and careers."

"That's her choice."

Sarah leaned her hip against the counter and

crossed her arms. "I know, but when I came here, I vowed to help the Amish without interfering in their way of life." She shrugged. "Maybe that was an unrealistic goal. Just by being here, I'm interfering."

"You're too hard on yourself."

Sarah turned back around and grabbed another dish out of the soapy water and began to scrub. "I had no idea that Amos kept such a tight rein on the family."

"The Amish are different."

Sarah grabbed a pair of glasses from the counter and placed them into the hot, soapy water. "Oh, I know. It's just that Temperance almost seemed frightened. Like a teenager who had done something wrong. I would have never invited them to the picnic if I had known it was going to be a problem."

Nick placed his hand on her arm. "You did nothing wrong. I know lots of Amish and *Englisch* who call each other friends and dine together." He frowned, realizing he could no longer delay telling her what had been on his mind.

"How did Mr. Zook feel about renting this house to you?"

Sarah slipped the dish towel from the oven handle and dried her hands. She leaned back on the counter, her forehead scrunched in concentration. "I hardly know the man. It has always been his wife, Temperance, and their children who I see. Temperance told me they decided to rent out the house for the extra money." She lifted a shoulder. "I don't suppose the breadwinner of the family would feel too good about his wife thinking he wasn't making enough."

"My thoughts exactly."

"You're not suggesting that Mr. Zook has been behind these…incidents," she said, apparently for lack of a better word.

Nick leaned against the counter next to Sarah, a clunky white drawer handle between them. "I don't think it's likely, but it's worth making note of."

"It has to be Jimmy. Or someone Jimmy hired."

"Unless," Nick said, truly grasping at straws, "Mr. Zook found my presence here to be yet another bad influence for his impressionable children, even though my presence is completely innocent."

Sarah crossed her arms and nodded. He detected a hint of pink creeping up her neck.

She pushed off the counter and pulled out a kitchen chair, the legs scraping loudly against the wood floor. She flopped down in it and stared at the dirty food trays stacked on the table. She bowed her head, and her long blond hair fell forward. He wanted nothing more than to take her into his arms and comfort her.

He pulled out a second chair and sat in front of her, their knees pressed against each other. "I didn't bring this up to stress you. Rather, I think we need to be vigilant. Maybe danger is closer than we thought."

Sarah tucked a long strand of hair behind her ear. "You think I attract this many crazies?"

A smile tugged at the corners of his mouth. "Do you think I'm crazy?"

She ran a hand through her hair and laughed. "You're the craziest of them all."

The next morning, Sarah still couldn't get Nick's concern regarding Amos Zook out of her head. She watched from the front window until she noticed him leave in his buggy. She had cleaned Temperance's tray—the one she had used to bring fresh corn to the picnic—and decided she'd return it as an excuse to stop over and chat.

Sarah told her mother she'd be right back and slipped out the door. Unease knotted her insides as she strode across the yard. Despite the heat, she chose to wear khakis and a long-sleeved top instead of shorts and a tank. If Amos happened to come home, she didn't want to give him more reason to be annoyed with her.

If he was annoyed with her. Maybe both she

and Nick had read too much into the Zook family's quick departure from the picnic last night. Maybe it was simply as Temperance had suggested—her husband liked a quiet meal at home with his family.

She lifted her hand to knock when the door swung open. Ruben stood in the doorway holding his little sister's hand. His eyebrows lifted in surprise. "I didn't know you were there."

Sarah laughed, but she felt like the joke was on her. "I hadn't had a chance to knock yet. I was bringing your mother's tray home." She lifted her arm and offered him the tray.

"I'll take that." Patience reached up and grabbed the dish. She spun around and ran toward the kitchen.

"Thank you. Is there anything else?" Ruben asked, a curious light in his dark eyes.

"I'm sorry things didn't work out with Mary Ruth."

Ruben immediately looked down and tapped the doorframe with his worn boot. He shrugged shyly. "I'll find someone else. But Mary Ruth is going to have a hard time." He looked up under the fringe of his bowl-cut hair. "Word's gotten around that she's spending too much time with outsiders."

Sarah's pulse kicked up a notch. "Are you referring to me?"

"You're not Amish, are you?"

Sarah jerked back her head, rather stunned. She hadn't expected such direct, rather rude, comments.

"Mary Ruth isn't doing anything wrong." Not that Sarah would guess. "She's been working with me. Honest work."

"The time for that has passed. She was supposed to be preparing for baptism and our marriage."

Sarah pressed her lips together as she struggled for the right thing to say. Had she always been conditioned to search for the right thing to say? To smooth things over?

"It's unfortunate that you feel that way. But—" it was Sarah's turn to shrug "—like you said, you'll find someone else. Mary Ruth will be fine." Sarah felt a sudden need to defend her sweet friend.

Ruben twisted his lips, and a flicker of something flashed in his eyes. Sarah was about to ask him if she had somehow offended him when his mother appeared behind him.

Temperance's gaze moved to the road and then back to Sarah as if she was worried her husband would return.

Sarah pointed toward the kitchen. "I returned your dish. Patience put it away."

"Denki." Temperance lifted her eyebrows in

expectation. "Is there something else? I have chores to do, and Ruben was going to take Patience into town for errands."

"Could I talk to you in private?"

A thin line creased Temperance's forehead. "Is something wrong?"

"I'll take Patience." Ruben disappeared into the house, and Temperance stepped onto the porch and closed the door behind her.

The floorboards of the front porch creaked under Sarah's steps. "I hope we didn't cause any trouble by inviting you to the picnic yesterday."

Temperance jerked her head back. "*Neh*, Amos was tired after his day at the auction. Our calves didn't fetch as much as he had hoped, so he was grumpy. Actually, the rent you pay helps tremendously right now."

"Are you sure everything is okay?" Sarah struggled to read the woman's guarded expression.

"*Yah*, everything is fine." Temperance reached for the door handle. "I'm sorry, but I have a lot of chores to do this morning. Please don't give it another thought."

"Okay." Sarah lingered for a moment before realizing Temperance wasn't going to open up to her. "Have a good day, then."

The Amish woman nodded and slipped back into the house. Sarah strolled across the yard, disappointed the meeting hadn't gone as she had hoped. Sarah stopped when she reached her porch and glanced back at her neighbor's home. She had the unnerving feeling that someone was watching her.

Insisting that Sarah not be without a vehicle while his truck was being fixed, Nick rented one for her. Initially, she resisted. He had already done so much for her. But now she was grateful. She had to run out for groceries. Her mother seemed especially tired this afternoon, and Sarah didn't want to leave her alone for long.

Sarah drove into the neighboring town and stocked up on groceries from a superstore. Tired yet relieved to have someone like Nick in her corner, Sarah made the drive back to her little home in the country.

The longer she was away from the house, the more she had a growing sense that something was wrong. She sent up a quick prayer that her mother was okay. Sarah hadn't left her mother alone for more than a few minutes here and there since she had moved in with her in Apple Creek. She prayed that nothing had happened to her in the two hours she was gone.

Sarah parked in front of the house and popped open the trunk. She grabbed the bags and headed toward the front door. She fumbled for the key, but something told her to try the handle. The door swung open.

Her heart dropped. She had distinctly locked it before she left. Maybe her mother had come outside to sit on the porch and then forgot to lock it again.

"Hello, Mom," Sarah called.

Silence except for the muffled sounds of barking.

She stepped into the room. Long shadows lingered in the corners. An episode of a familiar home-improvement show flickered on the corner TV set. Her mother was sitting in her recliner, her head angled in an awkward position.

Icy dread pulsed through Sarah's veins. She set the bags down on the floor and untwisted her hands from the wound-up plastic handles. "Mom?" she called again, hating the fear strangling her voice.

Sarah touched her mother's throat and said a prayer of thanks when she felt a steady pulse.

"She won't be up for a while."

Sarah's head snapped up. Jimmy stood in the doorway leading to the kitchen. Sarah backed up and tripped over the grocery bags and landed with an oomph.

Despite the sharp pain that shot up her spine, Sarah scrambled toward the door. Jimmy reached it first and slammed his hand against it. "Where do you think you're going?"

Her vision narrowed, a dark tunnel focused on his face. His mean, angry face. *How had I ever been attracted to this man? His ugliness radiates from his soul.*

"Don't do this, Jimmy. Let me go," Sarah pleaded, hating that she couldn't mask the fear in her voice.

"Are you going to leave your dear precious mother? And what about that rat of a dog I locked up in the bathroom? You know what I'm capable of."

"Please, leave us alone." She fought to keep the panic from her voice.

"Your mother was thirsty, so I ground up an extra dose of pain killers in her water. Now we can talk without being interrupted."

"I don't want to talk." Sarah jutted her chin out in a display of confidence she didn't feel.

Jimmy tilted his head. "That's obvious, since you took off without saying goodbye."

Sarah crossed her arms over her chest. Jimmy let his hot gaze travel the length of her.

"What? No thanks for looking out for your mother while you were gone and she was alone in Buffalo?"

Jimmy had stopped by to see her mother multiple times under the guise of checking up on her, but Sarah knew it was a ruse to find out where his former girlfriend was hiding.

"How did you find me?"

He stepped closer to her. "I'm a cop. It's what I do."

"You give cops a bad name." She blinked slowly, the rage building inside her. "Leave me and my mother alone. She deserves to spend her days in peace."

"If you didn't rip her away from one of the top treatment facilities, she wouldn't be counting down her last days. *Some* daughter you are." She could smell the alcohol on his breath. "Nice try, but I didn't believe your mother went to Florida for a minute. Keep asking enough questions, someone finally slips up. You can thank a new nurse who thinks I'm rather handsome."

Sarah's stomach knotted.

There it was, Jimmy doing what Jimmy did best. Persuading people. Trying to guilt her. But he wasn't going to succeed this time.

Her sole focus was to get rid of him. *Now.*

"Since you're standing next to the door, I suggest you leave," she bit out, trying to keep her jaw from trembling.

"Or what?" he asked in a tone Sarah suspected he first began to hone during his bullying days back in junior high.

Once a bully, always a bully.

"Jimmy, I don't want to be with you. There's no reason for you to be here."

He lifted his index finger and jabbed it in her face. "You humiliated me with my department."

Sarah squared off her shoulders. "*You lied.* You cost me my job. My friends. My home."

"You did it to yourself…" He took a step closer, his solid frame looming over her. "You can't be happy here in the sticks. Come home." His voice intended to be smooth, silky, convincing. Instead she heard it as grating, pathetic, annoying.

"I *am* home."

Hope sparked in her racing heart. *She's home.*

Jimmy let out a rough laugh. "Who's the guy?"

"There's no guy." The words rushed out before Sarah could think things through. Mean Jimmy was bad enough. Jealous Jimmy was ruthless.

"Don't lie to me. I saw his overnight kit in the bathroom." He lifted an eyebrow. "Unless you or your mother have taken to using a man's razor and aftershave."

Her mother stirred in the chair. Sarah struggled to look past Jimmy, but he grabbed her cheeks. "Look at me while I'm talking."

Sarah batted his hand away. Her jaw trembled, and she feared she wouldn't be able to get the words out. "He's here to protect me and my mother."

"From what?" Contempt dripped from his voice.

"You!" she screamed, losing patience. "From you! I'm sick of you terrorizing me." She charged him and shoved at his solid chest. He didn't budge. "Get. Out. Now."

Jimmy reached up and clutched her arms and set her aside, as if she were a rag doll. "What do you mean? Terrorizing you?"

"You've been hounding me for weeks."

Jimmy smiled, mocking her. "I have no idea what you're talking about. I didn't find your address until that dear, sweet nurse on your mother's hospital floor blurted out where you were. Must have been the uniform that convinced her to tell me." The smile slid from his face. Evil radiated from his eyes.

"I don't believe you. You've been harassing me and my mother."

"I only wanted to make sure your mother was okay. What, with you running off and all."

Sarah's pulse beat steadily in her ears. "Please leave," she said, defeat edging her plea.

"Nope, don't want to." Jimmy plopped down on the couch as if he owned the place. "Why don't you make me and your mother something to eat. I'm hungry. And get me a beer while you're at it."

Sarah slipped past him into the kitchen, not bothering to tell him she didn't have any beer.

"Don't try to call anyone or get any ideas. You might get away, but your mom won't."

Sarah pulled out a pot and filled it with water; her movements were on autopilot. She had no idea what she was going to make. Or how she was going to get out of this mess.

But one thing she knew for sure, she couldn't leave her mother alone with Jimmy. He'd likely kill her just to prove a point.

TWELVE

Nick was debating whether he should head to the diner for something to eat or risk showing up at Sarah's with an empty belly. He never wanted to presume he was a *regular* house-guest. He had a purpose. A job. To protect Sarah and her mother.

All indications pointed back to Jimmy. But until Jimmy messed up, Nick would have to keep doing his job. He had made a habit of ar-riving at Sarah's later in the evening so as not to intrude on her time with Maggie.

He didn't mind being her protector even if it involved sleeping on a lumpy cot in what must have once been a large pantry off the kitchen. He had caught a few z's in far rougher accom-modations.

Nick was still undecided on what he was going to do now that his shift was over when his cell phone rang. He pulled it out and frowned.

It was Matt, his friend who was keeping tabs on Jimmy.

"Yeah," Nick said, curtly.

"I have bad news. Jimmy's gone."

A knot twisted in his stomach. "What do you mean, he's gone?"

"Jimmy arrived for work. He's been on second shift recently. He parked behind the station and went in. I figured with the start of his shift, it was pretty safe to run and grab a bite to eat. When I came back, I noticed his truck was gone. I called one of my contacts at the station, and they said he went home sick." The private investigator's words seemed to be traveling through a long tunnel, getting further and further away.

"Let me guess. His truck's not at his house."

"No. I checked every location he's known to frequent. He's gone."

A muscle ticked in Nick's jaw. "Thanks for the heads-up. Call me if you find him." Nick ended the call and pressed his foot on the accelerator. There was no longer a question as to where he was headed.

When he reached Sarah's house, he pulled around back, scanning the landscape. That's when he saw it. The sun glinting off a piece of metal, the hood of a truck parked partially hidden by the barn. He shut off the ignition and climbed out.

Hand poised above his gun, he strode to the back porch. Nick poked his head around and saw a pot of water boiling on the stove.

He yanked open the screen door and cringed when it sent out a loud screech.

Jimmy stepped into the kitchen with an obnoxious smile on his face.

"What do we have here?" Jimmy asked, his words slurred. He glanced over his shoulder at something Nick couldn't see. "Your boyfriend's home."

"Jimmy, please, just leave." Sarah appeared behind Jimmy, a haggard expression on her face.

"Are you okay?" Nick asked, his hand lingering near his gun.

She blinked slowly, but didn't say anything.

Jimmy's gaze dropped to Nick's right hand. "What are you going to do, shoot me?" Jimmy rolled his eyes. His cheeks were flushed from drinking.

"The lady asked you to leave. I suggest you leave."

Jimmy twisted his lips. "I'll leave when I'm good and ready."

"I say you leave now." Nick took a step toward Sarah's former boyfriend. Jimmy blinked slowly, assessing the situation.

Jimmy smirked and sauntered toward the

door. "I'm leaving." He pointed a finger in Sarah's face. "But I'll be back."

Jimmy pushed out the screen door, and it slammed shut behind him. Nick watched as the man crossed the yard and got into his truck. The tires spit out gravel as he tore out of the driveway.

"Are you okay?" Nick asked, pulling a trembling Sarah into his embrace.

With her head against his chest, she nodded. Then she pushed him away and ran to her mother. She bent down and patted Maggie's hand. "Mom, Mom?"

The older woman stirred, but didn't open her eyes.

Sarah glanced over her shoulder at him, worry lines creasing the corners of her eyes. "We need to call Christina. Jimmy drugged my mom. She's been out of it since I arrived home."

Nick dialed his sister's number and spoke to Sarah while he waited for Christina to pick up. "Jimmy was here waiting for you?"

"Yeah," she said on a shaky breath.

Nick nodded and then spoke to his sister when she got on the line. Assured she'd be right over, he hung up and called the dispatch to pick up Jimmy. He didn't seem to be in any condition to drive.

"Mom?" Sarah called again.

Her mother turned her head and half opened her eyes. Certainly a good sign.

"How do you feel, Mom?"

"So…so…tired."

"Christina's on her way."

"That would be nice." Maggie was still groggy, but at least she was coming around.

Nick paced next to Sarah. "What did Jimmy say?"

"Same old story. He wants me to come home. I kept asking him to leave."

"I should have been here," he scolded himself.

Sarah touched his arm. "I'm okay. You came when it counted." Then she cocked her head. "How did you know?"

"Matt called me when he realized Jimmy was missing." Nick rubbed his jaw. "Did Jimmy tell you how he found you?"

"Yes, but it can't be the whole truth. He claimed he got the info that my mom was here with me from a nurse at the hospital. But he knew I was here all along."

She shook her head, a distant look in her eyes. "He's been harassing me well before my mother ended up in the hospital."

"He's a known liar."

"I know. I learned that the hard way." She dragged a hand across her hair. "Am I going to have to move with my mother?" Her gaze drifted over to Maggie.

Nick's heart sank. He couldn't ask her to stay on account of him. But, then again, he couldn't protect her if she moved away from Apple Creek.

Sarah could finally breathe again when Christina showed up and assured her that Maggie would be fine. Groggy, but fine. Sarah and Christina helped Maggie into bed. Lola climbed in next to her. It seemed they both needed reassurance after their stressful day.

The rest of them returned to the sitting room. Tension rolled off Nick as he paced the small space, making and taking phone calls. It seemed that all his fellow officers were on the lookout for Jimmy's truck.

Nick was like a caged animal, ready to strike but confined to this place to protect Sarah in case Jimmy made his way back here as he had promised.

Jimmy's angry face was seared in her memory. He had left drunk and in a blind rage.

Nick opened his mouth to say something when his phone rang again. He held up a finger, then turned his back to take the call. Sarah listened—her heart thudding in her chest—as Nick gave a series of quick, one-word answers.

When he turned back around, all the color had drained from his face.

Sarah's blood turned icy cold in her veins. She wanted to ask him what was wrong, but the words got tangled in a knot of emotion.

"That was Sheriff Maxwell."

"What's going on, Nick?" Christina spoke up for both of them.

"There's been an accident."

Pinpricks of panic raced across Sarah's flesh. She lowered herself onto the arm of the couch. "Jimmy?" The single word squeaked out. "Did he hurt someone?"

Nick crouched down in front of her and pulled her hands into his. Sarah lifted her gaze to Christina, who had a hand pressed to her mouth. Sarah met Nick's gaze and pleaded with her eyes to tell her what was going on.

"He crashed into a tree. Barely missed Ruben Zook in his wagon on the way back from town."

"Oh, no," Sarah breathed.

Nick squeezed her hands. "Ruben's fine." They locked gazes, and Sarah knew what he had to say before he said it.

"Jimmy's dead."

The walls swayed, and sweat broke out on her brow. Sarah pushed to her feet and felt light-headed. She touched the back of her mother's recliner to steady herself. "Are they sure?"

"Yes."

A myriad of emotions playing out on Nick's handsome face. But most of all she saw compassion.

Sarah lifted her hand to cover her heart. "God forgive me, but I feel relieved. Is my nightmare finally over?"

A sad smile slanted the corners of Nick's mouth. "Jimmy Braeden won't be causing anyone any more trouble ever again."

THIRTEEN

Sarah brought her mother tea out on the front porch, where she sat in a rocker. "How do you feel this morning?" She set the tea down on the small side table. A few days had passed since Jimmy's fatal accident, and Sarah was still trying to get her head around it.

Her mother's chest expanded. "I don't know what it is about the country air, but I feel good." She covered her mouth and coughed. She leaned over and took a sip of the tea and waved her hand, apparently registering the concern on her daughter's face. "I'm fine. Just a little tickle in my throat."

They both knew it was more than a tickle, but her mother seemed to be enjoying her respite in the country.

"This place sure is quiet without Nick here," her mother said, changing the subject.

"Well, with Jimmy..." Sarah struggled to acknowledge his death. He had been a dark cloud hanging over her for so long.

Jimmy was really gone. Dead.

"Now that Jimmy can't hurt me, Nick doesn't have to protect us."

She traced the rim of her teacup. "Nick'll be missed. He's a good guy."

Sarah recalled the few phone calls Nick had made to her since Jimmy had driven his truck into a tree. Their conversations had been cordial, but always skirted around what was now at the forefront of her mind—could she and Nick have a future?

Why? What's the point? She'd be leaving Apple Creek soon.

"I've been thinking," her mother said.

"Sounds like trouble." Sarah laughed as she sat down next to her. There was a certain sadness in her heart knowing that Jimmy had lost his life. He had been a miserable man, but he was still someone's son and brother. Needless to say, she didn't go to the funeral or make contact with his family. They would feel nothing toward her but blame.

Even though her rational side told her he had brought this downfall upon himself. Her soft heart couldn't help but feel she had been partially responsible.

She knew it was ridiculous. She hoped time could heal all wounds, as they said.

"Are you going to tell me what you're thinking about?" Sarah asked.

"Staying here." Her mother tapped the arms of the rocking chair. "Right here."

Sarah made a funny face. "On the front porch?"

"You are a funny girl. No, right here in Apple Creek. It's peaceful. I feel good out here. The old house back home reminds me too much of all the sadness in our lives. This place feels fresh. Like new possibilities." A smile tugged at the corner of her mother's mouth. "Or maybe it's the fresh-cut grass I smell." She tilted her head and glanced at the farm next door. "I love watching the Amish family work. It's fascinating. It beats watching the soap operas and Mr. Davidson next door to the old house walk that yappy dog of his." Lola lifted her head as if she knew what they were talking about, then settled back down.

"Oh, Trinket—" Mr. Davidson's Jack Russell terrier "—wouldn't hurt a fly."

"I know. But that old man didn't do the dog any favors by not training him." Mostly her mother didn't appreciate Mr. Davidson not cleaning up after the small dog. Sarah couldn't blame her. "So, what do you think? Should we stay in Apple Creek for a little bit longer? Maybe until winter?"

Sarah thought of the poor clients in the rural countryside, the young struggling Amish and Nick. A spark of hope blossomed in her heart. "It's something we could consider," she said noncommittally when her heart was thumping, *yes, yes, yes.*

Sarah closed her eyes and tipped her head, resting it against the rocker. The sun warmed her face. She started to doze, then startled awake. She blinked a few times as the cornfield swayed in her line of vision. She no longer had anything to fear.

Jimmy was gone.

Yet a whisper of dread tickled her brain. *What if Jimmy hadn't been the only one harassing me?* She shook away the thought, figuring a person couldn't live under the constant threat of harm for so long without suffering negative aftereffects.

Jimmy's gone. Relax.

A few days later, Sarah said goodbye to the last young Amish man from her Sunday-night meeting in the church basement, then turned to Mary Ruth. "Let's leave the sweeping for another day."

Mary Ruth set the broom aside and smiled. "Sounds good."

"Come here, sit down."

Mary Ruth's eyes widened and her cheeks grew flushed as if she had done something wrong.

Sarah smiled. "I want to talk. So much has gone on, and I wanted to make sure you're okay."

Mary Ruth's hand flew to her chest. "You want to make sure I'm doing okay?" She angled her head in disbelief. "How are *you*?"

Sarah paused and gave her answer thoughtful consideration. "I'm doing well. I've done a lot of praying about Jimmy and realize he made his own choices."

"And how is Deputy Nick Jennings?"

Sarah reached over and playfully tugged on Mary Ruth's dress, the long fabric draping over her legs. "You've been talking to my mother."

"I love visiting with your mother. You're lucky to have her. My *mem* has been giving me what you'd call the cold shoulder since I called things off with Ruben. I suppose she assumes there are...what is the expression?...no more fish in the sea."

Mary Ruth's joke didn't mask the sadness radiating off her.

Sarah looked her young Amish friend in the

eye. "Don't feel pressure to do anything you don't want to do."

Mary Ruth laughed, a shy awkward noise. "You sound like you're talking to the group about drugs or alcohol."

"I suppose that advice holds true for a lot of things. If you're not sure about your future, give it some prayerful consideration."

"Amish life isn't like *Englisch* life. Most of my friends are married. One is expecting a baby already." Sarah thought she detected a whiff of longing in Mary Ruth's voice.

"Is that what you want?"

"Someday, sure. But—" Mary Ruth shrugged "—I'm not sure. It seems my parents are harder on me ever since my brother left Apple Creek."

"Tell me, how would your life be different if your brother had stayed?"

"For one, my parents wouldn't be so focused on me all the time. I'm their second-oldest kid. I think they're having nightmares about how bad it will reflect on them if another one of their kids leaves."

Sarah reached out and caught Mary Ruth's hands. "Stop worrying about everyone else. What do you want to do?"

Mary Ruth blinked slowly. "I don't know."

"And that's okay." Sarah squeezed her hands. "Give yourself time."

Mary Ruth pulled her hands away and swiped at her long dress in a self-conscious gesture.

"Is that what you're doing?" Mary Ruth asked, her voice barely a whisper.

"What do you mean?"

"Giving yourself time to figure things out? Deputy Jennings sure seems to be sweet on you."

It was Sarah's turn to squirm in her chair. "My focus is on my mom."

"I've talked to your mom. She'd like you to channel some of that focus on something else."

Sarah laughed. "I guess I've been a bit of a hoverer."

"Like I said, you and your mom are lucky to have one another."

"You'd think she'd be bored at the house all day, but she enjoys being out in the country."

"Didn't you guys used to do some crafts? Maybe you could do that."

Excitement bubbled up in Sarah's chest. "That's a great idea. I should collect some of the flowers growing by the creek, and we could dry them out and make a wreath for the door."

"Sounds like fun. I could also teach your mom how to quilt."

Sarah nodded. "Sounds like a great idea." She tilted her head toward the door. "Should we call it a night?"

"Yah," Mary Ruth said, her Pennsylvania Dutch slipping through.

They climbed the stairs and pushed the door open, stepping out onto the church parking lot. Sarah turned the key in the door.

"Want a ride home?" Sarah asked. She had picked up a secondhand car recently. Reliable and affordable.

"I better walk. I don't want to give Mem or Dat a reason to scold me tonight."

Sarah lifted her hand and waved to the pastor's wife standing in the window with the curtain pulled back.

Turning her attention back to Mary Ruth, Sarah said, "Honoring your father and mother is a good thing, a very good thing. But you need to pray on your own future. God wants you to be happy, too."

Mary Ruth tipped her head shyly. "The *Englischers'* ways are so very different than Amish ways."

"I know, and I could never understand what it means to be Amish. So, please, consider that when you weigh my advice." Sarah lifted her eyebrows to emphasize the point.

"I hope you're praying on your future, too."

"Prayer is my constant companion," Sarah muttered.

"Then I think you're not listening too hard,

because there's no way God would bring a man like Deputy Jennings into your life and expect you not to grab hold and start a new future." Mary Ruth lifted her eyebrows, mimicking Sarah.

"I'm the trained professional." Sarah forced a laugh, referring to her degree in social work.

"Fancy college degrees aren't necessary when it comes to affairs of the heart." It was Mary Ruth's turn to tip her head and study her friend closely.

Sarah shook her head and walked over to her car. The sun was hanging low on the horizon. "You'll want to hurry home before it gets dark."

Mary Ruth waved and strode across the parking lot toward the dark country road leading to her family's farm. Sarah started the car and pulled up alongside her. "Are you sure you don't want a ride?"

Mary Ruth hesitated for a moment, then scrunched up her face. "*Neh*, best if I hurry along."

Sarah sat in the car and watched her friend. Guilt rankled her for allowing the girl to walk home alone. But then again, it wasn't Sarah's choice. The young woman had a lot of choices to make for herself. Difficult ones that her Amish family may or may not agree with—depending on the road she took.

Another thought whispered across Sarah's brain. *Maybe I really am needed in Apple Creek*. One thing she knew for sure: when she left Apple Creek, she'd really miss it.

Nick's sister claimed the low-tire-pressure indicator kept popping on in her car's dash despite having put more air in the tire last night. Now, she needed a ride to check on Maggie. Nick suspected her car troubles were Christina's sly attempt at matchmaking.

Nick didn't mind. He hadn't seen Sarah in a few days, and time was slipping away. He couldn't help but fear Sarah and her mother would be moving back to Buffalo soon.

When Nick stepped through the front door behind his sister, he noticed Sarah look up from her book on the couch, a smile brightening her face.

His heart stuttered in his chest. *Man, he had missed her*.

"Good afternoon," Christina said cheerfully. "How is everyone doing?"

Sarah placed her book facedown on the side table to hold her page. "Hello. Fine, thanks. I didn't realize it had gotten so late." She blinked a few time as if trying to focus after being lost in a good book for a long time.

Maggie sat next to Mary Ruth at a large piece

of fabric stretched across a wood frame. "We're doing great. Mary Ruth is teaching me how to quilt. By hand!" Maggie raised the thread and needle eye level and smiled. "Not with one of those fancy machines my friend Barbara is always going on about. The workmanship in this is incredible." She beamed with pride.

Nick leaned in to study the fabric. "Nice. Very nice." His gaze drifted to Sarah, and she glanced away.

Christina put her medical bag down on the table and studied her patient. "You do look well. The question is, how do you feel?"

"It feels great to be away from the hospital and all the treatments." She slipped the needle through the fabric to keep it in place. She set her hands in her lap. "You don't have to run out here. I promise I'll call if I'm not feeling well."

Suddenly realizing what she had said, Maggie threw up her hands. "Of course, we'd love to have either of the Jenningses visit us at any time, but it doesn't have to be an official visit."

Sarah drifted into the kitchen while Christina and Maggie chatted about her health. Nick followed her.

Sarah turned on the faucet and filled half the sink with soapy water. She set a few dishes in the water and turned around.

Nick held up his hand toward the sitting room. "My sister needed a ride."

"That was nice of you."

"I haven't seen you in town lately."

Sarah pulled her hair into a ponytail and wrapped an elastic band around it. She slumped back against the counter. "I've been seeing a few clients, but mostly I've been spending time with Mom."

"I'm glad you can enjoy this time in peace."

Sarah bowed her head and wiped at a tear that had trailed down her face. She pressed her lips together. Nick wanted to pull her into an embrace. To tell her everything was going to be okay. But it wasn't his place.

And it wasn't a promise he could make.

"I've spent so long running away from Jimmy that I missed precious time with my mom."

Nick swallowed hard, his heart breaking for her. "What's important is the time you have now."

Sarah looked up, her eyes shiny with tears. "It's hard. I still can't seem to totally let my guard down."

Nick cleared his throat. "How long do you plan to stay in Apple Creek?" He finally asked the question that had been heavy on his mind.

"Until the weather gets bad. My mom likes it here."

"It's not a bad place." Nick ran the back of his knuckles across her cheek.

Her face flushed.

"My parents were in town for a few days. They come home every so often to recharge, as they like to say."

Sarah brushed past him and sat down at the kitchen table. "Where are they now?"

"Jetted off to Paris." He waved his hand. "Or some other international city. They're semiretired now, so most of their travel they claim is for leisure. But knowing my parents, they've got their hands in different business ventures."

"I would have liked to meet them." She dragged her hand down her ponytail. "How did two wealthy entrepreneurs raise a police officer?"

"What about my sister the small-town doctor?"

Sarah raised her eyebrows. "But she's still a doctor." She laughed and shook her head.

"You need to meet our little sister, Kelly," Christina wandered into the kitchen. "Smarter than both of us combined."

Nick laughed. "Thanks, sis."

Christina smirked. "Hey, if Sarah hasn't already realized what a numskull you are, then… well, then I underestimated her."

Sarah rubbed the back of her neck, obviously feeling self-conscious.

"Ready to go?" Christina asked Nick.

He nodded, then turned to Sarah. "Hope to see you again soon."

Sarah stood. "Thanks for taking such good care of my mom. We both appreciate it."

"You're welcome." Christina squeezed Sarah's arm. "Make sure you take care of yourself, too."

Christina turned and grabbed her brother's arm. "Let's go."

Once they got outside and into his car, Christina didn't give him a chance to start the car before she started in on him. "If you let Sarah Gardner go, you're a bigger idiot than—"

"Sisterly love," he muttered.

Nick turned the key in the ignition and headed out onto the country road.

"Sarah's not Amber. You need to move past her."

Nick cut her a sideways glance. "You think I'm still pining away for Amber?" Forced disgust edged his tone.

"No, she wasn't right for you. But I think you're afraid of taking a chance. Amber said she'd wait for you when you were deployed. But she didn't. Now you're afraid to make a commitment to Sarah because you're…oh, I know… you're afraid she's going to leave."

"She *is* going to leave." Nick ran a hand over his jaw. "Besides, she's had her fill of cops."

"You're not like her former boyfriend. Any more than she's like your former girlfriend."

Nick tapped his fingers on the steering wheel. "It's not going to work."

"You know best," his sister said in the way little sisters talked to big brothers. "Like always." Sarcasm dripped from her voice. "But relationships—solid relationships—don't come around that often."

"Perhaps you should work on your own personal life," Nick said, feeling defensive.

"When I'm not saving the world," Christina replied in a mocking tone. "When I'm not saving the world."

FOURTEEN

After enjoying a late dinner of takeout pizza, Mary Ruth and Sarah's mother went back to quilting. "Wow, you guys are determined." Sarah ran a finger over the delicate stitching.

"It's relaxing. You should try it," Maggie suggested. "Besides, what better thing to do on a rainy day?" The past few days had been rainy, and the two women had made a lot of progress on their quilt.

Mary Ruth looked up. "I'm enjoying this single life. If I were married, my husband would be looking for dinner and I'd probably be doing dishes—" she got a faraway look "—chasing after a toddler."

Maggie made a tsk-tsk sound. "Marriage is more than cooking dinner and doing dishes." She shook her head briefly as if stopping herself from saying more. "Just you wait until you meet the right man. A man who makes your heart go pitter-patter." Her mother met Sarah's gaze and lifted an eyebrow.

"Really now, Mom. Can we have one night where you guys aren't hounding me about Nick?"

"So, he *does* make your heart go pitter-patter." Mary Ruth broke down in a laughing fit, her porcelain cheeks turning a bright red.

"You guys joke all you want. I'm going to stretch my legs. I need to work off all that pizza. Anyone want to join me?"

"This quilt's not going to make itself." Her mother tilted her head back and looked at the stitching through her readers.

"I'll be back shortly. The rain's let up for now."

Sarah slipped on a light jacket, and Lola jumped at her feet, eager to go outside. Once on the back porch, Sarah admired the magnificent view. Instead of walking along the country road—she had spent enough time doing that during the months she was trying to stay under Jimmy's radar—she decided to take a walk along the property's edge and farther along the creek. Maybe she'd find some of those wildflowers she promised to get so her mom could make a wreath. She hoped it wasn't too wet. Either way, she'd collect a nice bouquet of flowers.

Lola enjoyed exploring every inch of the path.

The creek was babbling and racing downstream like Sarah had never seen it before. There were talks of floods in the next county.

As the long grass tickled the back of her legs, she tuned in to her strong muscles. Having lived with her mother these past few weeks made her appreciate every moment. Every full breath.

Pushing her shoulders back, Sarah strode farther along the edge of the creek. The rush of the water filled her ears. She understood why her mother was so at peace here.

Can I stay in Apple Creek?

Apprehension and a bubble of excitement swirled in her belly.

Should she take the risk?

The creek edged the back of the Zooks' property and disappeared through the woods. She had never ventured this far, but she was enjoying being alone with her thoughts and was curious where the path led. She decided she'd follow it a little way until the bugs got to be too much.

As she followed the trail along the creek, she swatted at a few insects swarming around her head. "Maybe we should turn back," she said to the dog. "It's awfully buggy out here."

A twig snapped behind her, and she spun around and came up short. Ruben was standing in her path. The way he stared at her made her skin crawl, far more than any bugs flitting around her face.

"You should have turned back a long time ago," he said, his voice even. Lola yapped at his feet.

"I'm..." Her head swirled in confusion. "What do you need, Ruben?"

Ruben pushed the dog aside with his foot, and Sarah opened her mouth to protest when he took a step toward her. Instinctively, Sarah took a step back. A million crushing moments flashed through her brain. Moments when Jimmy had intimidated her. Had kept her in her place. Had chased her away.

But Jimmy was dead.

And here another man made the same horrible feeling snake up her spine.

"I'm walking on my property," Ruben answered with a snarl.

Panic bit her fingertips and raced up her arms. Lola's incessant barking amped up her alarm. "Excuse me. I have to get back." She attempted to brush past Ruben when his arm snaked out and caught her wrist.

"You should have left a long time ago."

Sarah yanked her arm, but Ruben tightened his grip.

"Let go!" she demanded. She forced a confidence in her voice that she didn't feel.

"*No*. You should have left Apple Creek a long time ago. What does it take?" He gritted his teeth. "I've tried everything. A dead snake. Pushing you off the ladder."

Sarah gasped and tried desperately to wrench out of his grasp.

"*Yah*, well…you're going now." Ruben took his other hand and shoved her shoulder and let go of her wrist at the same time. Sarah lost her footing and tumbled into the swollen creek. The last thing she saw before the black water swallowed her up was Ruben's icy gaze.

Nick had been thinking nonstop about Sarah these past few days. When he arrived home and glanced around, he had a startling realization: he had a house. It had everything he needed to live, but it never felt like home.

When do I most feel at home?

The answer hit him like a bullet between his eyes. He felt like home with Sarah. He dropped into the oversize chair parked in front of the television and picked up the remote, but he didn't turn it on. That's all he did when he was home. Watch TV. He supposed it was his way of avoiding the loneliness.

Nick leaned over and opened the drawer in the side table. He pulled out a framed photo of him and Amber that had been taken at the airport, him in his army fatigues, Amber in her skinny jeans and sweater, an expensive handbag hanging over her arm.

He had cared for her, but even before he got a Dear John letter from her when he was hunkered down in a tent in the middle of the desert, he had sensed it was over. Sure, the way she had done it tore his heart out.

What kind of woman broke up with her boyfriend when he was on a tour of duty? And it reinforced some trust issues.

But Sarah wasn't Amber.

Nick had been blinded by the type of women he met in his parents' affluent circles. But Sarah was the kind of woman he could fall in love with…

Fall in love…

Nick tossed the framed photo back in the table drawer and slammed it shut. He got to his feet, hurried to change his clothes, then grabbed his car keys from the table.

Nick had to tell her how he felt before she left Apple Creek for good.

For a man who claimed to have nerves of steel under a stressful situation, Nick Jennings thought his heart was going to race out of his chest as he stood on Sarah's porch with a bouquet of wildflowers in his hand.

He knocked and Mary Ruth answered. Her eyes dropped to the flowers in his hand and amusement danced in her eyes. "Hello, Deputy Jennings."

"Hello. Is Sarah here?"

"Who's here?" Maggie called from inside the house.

"It's Deputy Jennings. I think he's sweet on our Sarah."

Maggie appeared behind Mary Ruth, a colorful bandanna wrapped around her head. "Well, it's about time." She smiled and reached around Mary Ruth to squeeze his arm. "Sarah went for a walk. I expect her back any minute." Maggie waved her arm. "Come in. Wait for her."

Nick rolled up on the balls of his feet. He couldn't wait inside. He'd go stir-crazy. "Where does she normally walk?" He hadn't noticed Sarah walking along the road on his drive over.

Mary Ruth smiled and pointed with her thumb toward the back of the house. "I believe she took a walk along the creek."

"Thanks. I'll be right back."

"Be good to my daughter," Maggie hollered after Nick as he pivoted on his heel and jogged down the steps, still holding on to the flowers. He figured the flowers would be an ice breaker when the right words wouldn't come. Besides, he didn't want an audience, even if it was in the form of sweet Maggie and Mary Ruth. What he had to say was between him and Sarah.

A nervous bubble exploded in his gut, and he picked up his pace before he lost his nerve.

Some tough guy.

He jogged around to the back of the house and followed the path until he reached the woods. He swatted at the mosquitos buzzing around his head.

In the distance he could hear barking.

Alarm spiked his pulse.

Nick wanted to call out to Sarah, but something kept him silent. He tossed the bouquet of flowers aside and ran. Something in his gut told him Sarah was in danger. Lola wouldn't be barking like that otherwise.

The gray shadows of dusk hovered over the path. The creek churned on his right, angry from the constant rains of the past few days.

Around the first bend, an Amish man in a straw hat held a long branch in his hands and was beating at something in the creek.

Instinctively, Nick's hand hovered over the gun he always carried on his belt, even when he was off duty. "What's going on?"

The man turned his head, and Nick recognized him. Ruben Zook. He lived on the neighboring farm. Nick's posture relaxed, but then a trickle of unease wound its way up his spine when he tuned in to Ruben's angry gaze. Lola barked frantically at something in the creek.

"Get out of here." Ruben lunged toward Nick.

With one hand on his gun and the other out in front of him, Nick shouted, "Step back."

A bloodcurdling scream ripped from down below, along the steep edge of the creek.

"What's going on?" Nick repeated, easing his gun out of the holster and pointing it at the young Amish man.

"She ruined my life by putting stupid ideas in Mary Ruth's head."

Nick's finger twitched, millimeters from the trigger. He didn't have to ask who *she* was. His heart pulsing in his ear, Nick grabbed Ruben's stick and shoved the Amish man, making him land on his backside. Nick tossed the stick aside and handcuffed Ruben to get him out of the way.

Nick jabbed his finger in his face. "Don't move."

Nick proceeded to the edge of the creek near Lola, careful that the earth didn't crumble underneath his footing. "Sarah!" he called, but all he saw in the gathering dark was the churning waters.

"Sarah!"

With trembling hands he flicked on the flashlight on his cell phone and scanned the waters. He glanced over his shoulder at Ruben, who was sniveling under his straw hat.

"Did she go into the creek?"

"Good riddance," Ruben muttered.

"Sarah!" The swollen creek could have carried her a long way down. But instead of running downstream, something kept him there. He moved the beam of the flashlight along the tangle of tree branches lining the edge, and that's when he saw her.

Sarah was caught up in the branches. Her face pale. Her eyes closed. Her lips blue.

His heart sank.

Dear Lord, please give me the strength to save her. Let her be okay.

Nick slid down the embankment. Holding on to a root, he leaned precariously over the raging creek toward Sarah. With all his strength, he pulled her toward him and out of the water. "I gotcha. I gotcha."

Help me, Lord.

He put Sarah over his shoulder in a fireman's hold and used the branch to pull himself back up to the pathway. He laid her down gently and smoothed her wet hair out of her eyes.

Nick gave Ruben a quick glance. He had the good sense to stay seated. Anger heated Nick's wet skin.

He checked her airway. Clear.

He watched the quiet rise and fall of her chest.

He felt Sarah's neck for a pulse. It beat steady. *Thank You, Lord.*

Nick leaned in close to the woman he had grown to love. "Sarah... Sarah..."

She groaned. The most beautiful sound he had ever heard. She struggled, then pushed up on her elbow and hung her head, sputtering and coughing.

"Ruben..."

"I know. He's not going anywhere."

Sarah tried to sit up, and Nick wrapped his arm around her to help her to a seated position. Her body trembled despite the humid evening. "Why are you here?" She lifted her eyes to meet his.

"I came here to talk to you." The reason could wait.

Sarah lifted her hand and patted his cheek. "Good thing for me..."

"No—" he ran the pad of his thumb across her wet cheek "—good thing for me." Nick bent down and scooped her up. "Let's get you to the house."

"I can walk."

"I know. But let me do this for you."

Sarah nodded and rested her head on his shoulder.

Nick barked out orders to Ruben to stand and follow them. Nick wasn't in the mood for nonsense.

And good thing for Ruben, he followed Nick's instructions.

Lola ran ahead to the house.

When they reached the back porch, Nick ordered Ruben to sit on the lawn. He carried Sarah up the porch steps and kicked the door to get Mary Ruth or Maggie's attention.

Mary Ruth appeared at the door. "What happened?" She pushed open the door, and Nick slipped in with Sarah in his arms. Lola scooted in and curled up on the couch.

Mary Ruth grabbed a quilt from the back of the couch. Nick put Sarah down, and the young Amish girl wrapped the quilt around Sarah's shoulders.

Sarah looked up at Nick, her lips quivering. "I need to change and get out of these wet clothes."

"Are you okay? Should I call my sister?"

"I'm fine. Thanks to you." She pulled the quilt tighter around her neck and a shiver shook her body. She turned to Mary Ruth. "It was Ruben. He tried to chase me out of town."

Mary Ruth's face grew pale, and she shook her head slowly. "Ruben's been harassing you?" Her lips trembled. "I'm sorry."

Sarah touched her friend's arm. "It's not your

fault. We all have to take responsibility for our own actions."

Nick smiled. Seemed Sarah had finally realized she wasn't responsible for Jimmy's horrendous behavior.

"What brought you out to the path?"

"Go change and then I'll tell you."

Sarah smiled and tossed the quilt down on the couch and with Mary Ruth's assistance, went for dry clothes.

Maggie approached Nick, wide-eyed. "What happened?"

"Turns out it was Ruben Zook who has been harassing Sarah."

"Harassing her? Why? He pushed her into the creek?" The questions flowed out one after the other without waiting for an answer.

"He blames her for losing Mary Ruth." Nick squeezed Maggie's hand. "Sarah's fine."

"Thanks to you."

"I need to call the sheriff's station. Have someone take Ruben in." Nick looked through the screen door. Ruben sat with his head bowed. He seemed truly deflated.

FIFTEEN

After Sarah changed into warm, dry clothes, she found Mary Ruth sitting between Nick and her mother on the couch. Lola curled up on Maggie's lap. Sarah lingered in the doorway watching Mary Ruth bent over, sobbing, her face in her hands.

Her mother patted the Amish girl's back, and Nick seemed uncomfortable. Sarah shifted her feet and caught Nick's eye. He stood and held out his arm, gesturing for her to have his seat on the couch.

As she brushed past him, Nick placed his hand on the small of her back and whispered, "You look much better. You doing okay?"

Warmth coiled around her heart. "Yes, thanks to you." She kept her voice low, feeling a little disrespectful with Mary Ruth in tears on the couch. "I can't thank you enough."

Nick glanced over at Mary Ruth as Sarah's

mother handed her a tissue. "I'm glad God put me in the right place at the right time."

"I am, too." Then Sarah looked around, suddenly concerned. "Where's Ruben?"

"The sheriff picked him up. When you're ready, we can go to the station and file a report."

Sarah nodded and joined Mary Ruth on the couch. Sarah leaned close to her friend's ear. "Everything's going to be okay."

Mary Ruth straightened and drew in a shuddering breath. "Ruben wasn't the right man for me, but I never thought he was evil."

"Sometimes people become unhinged when they love someone." Sarah's thoughts went to Jimmy. "Let me rephrase that: they do crazy things for what they think is love. That's not love. You were smart to kick him to the curb."

Mary Ruth swiped at her tears. "My family didn't think so."

"Your parents want you to live your life in the Amish community. They thought Ruben was your future. But they couldn't have known he had...issues," she said, for lack of a better word. "I'm sure you and your family will reconcile and eventually you'll meet another nice Amish boy."

Mary Ruth wiped her nose. Her whole body shook from a mix of laughter and tears. "I'm not getting any younger. Where will I meet someone?"

"There's nothing wrong with spending a little time getting to know yourself." Sarah looked up and met Nick's gaze and then quickly dropped it to Mary Ruth's trembling hands. "You've had a terrible shock today. Give it time. Have faith."

Mary Ruth reached out and clutched Sarah's hand. "Look at me bawling like a fool. You're the one who nearly drowned. How can you ever forgive me for putting you in this position?"

"It's not your fault. You didn't do these things to me. Ruben did." A little voice niggled at the back of her head. All this time she had been bashing herself for all her bad choices and how she had ruined her life. But her only mistake had been trusting Jimmy. From there, his bad choices had been his own.

Sarah closed her eyes and breathed in deeply. Despite the horrible day, she felt like a weight had been lifted. Just like she had told Mary Ruth to let it go and move on, to not blame herself, Sarah had to do the same.

Sarah was only responsible for her own choices. Her eyes lifted and she met Nick's gaze. And in the scheme of life, she had made some wonderful choices.

Nick drove Mary Ruth home. When they reached her house, he offered to go in and explain the circumstances surrounding Ruben's arrest.

Mary Ruth shook her bonneted head. "*Neh*, it's time that I spoke to my parents. Really spoke to them. There's been a lot of tension since I called things off with Ruben. If I bring law enforcement in, it won't set the right tone." She hesitated a moment. "I'm sorry."

"No, don't be. I understand."

Mary Ruth nodded and pulled the handle, and the dome light popped on. "The benefit of the rumor mill in Apple Creek is that I probably won't have to tell them much. I'm sure they've already heard." She shook her head. "Well, they've probably heard a version of the truth."

Nick turned around in the driveway and as promised, headed back to Sarah's house. He had left her to chat with her mother. They both needed reassurance after what happened tonight. Ostensibly, he needed to bring her to the station for her official statement, but more important, he needed to tell Sarah what had brought him to her home earlier tonight in the first place.

When he arrived at her house, he was surprised to find Sarah sitting in the front-porch rocker. Nick climbed out of his car and strolled toward her. The moonlight glinted in the whites of her eyes. He placed his foot on the bottom step and rested his elbow on the railing.

"Mom was tired. She went to bed." Sarah answered the unasked question.

"Good. I'm sure she'll sleep well."

Sarah lifted her eyebrows. "I know I will."

"The first time I came over tonight—" Nick shifted the conversation, eager to say what he had been waiting to say all night "—I had a bouquet of wildflowers in my hand."

She rocked the chair by pushing her bare toes on the wood slats. "Likely story."

"Really. I did. But then I had to rescue someone."

"Someone? Really? So, you're a hero?" She pushed to her feet and crossed over to him. Nick climbed another step. She stopped at the top step looking down at him.

"I wouldn't call myself a hero."

"I would." She reached out and cupped his cheek, her warm fingers sending tingles of awareness through him. "How can I possibly thank you for being there for me tonight?" Sarah's voice cracked over the last words. "I don't want to think what could have…" she shook her head, and a shudder traveled through her body.

"Are you cold? Maybe you should go inside."

Sarah shook her head again. "It's a beautiful evening."

Nick wrapped his hand around her wrist and kissed the palm of her hand. She smelled fresh and clean from the shower after her dip in the creek.

Nick led her to the wicker love seat at the far end of the porch.

He tracked the lines on the palm of her hand. "I came over earlier tonight to tell you how much I cared about you. How I hoped you'd stay in Apple Creek. How I hoped we could make a serious go at—" he flicked his fingers in the air between them "—whatever this is between us. I mean, I've had trust issues. My last girlfriend…" Suddenly, he found himself rambling.

He had finally realized he couldn't let the hurt from his past relationship with Amber influence his future happiness. Sarah was nothing like Amber.

The pulse in his ears grew louder, drowning out his words. *Why isn't she saying anything?* Maybe it was too soon. Maybe he was…

Sarah leaned closer and brushed a kiss across his lips. She pulled back and stared deeply into his eyes. "I promised myself I'd never date another cop."

"I—"

Sarah pressed her index finger against his lips and smiled. "When I made that promise, I didn't know you." She pulled away her hand and traced his jawline with her thumb. "I have never met someone as caring as you. I would love to take the time to get to know you better." Her eyes lingered on his. "You can trust me."

"I know." A weight lifted from Nick's heart. "Does that mean you'll be staying in Apple Creek?"

Sarah glanced toward the door. "My mom loves it here. And full-confession mode—" she smiled brightly "—I do, too."

Nick took Sarah's face in both his hands and gave her a proper kiss. "I love you." He kissed her again, and he felt her lips curve against his into a smile.

Sarah wrapped both her hands around his wrists and beamed up at him. "I love you, too."

EPILOGUE

14 months later...

Nick arrived home from work and strode through the empty house. He reached the back door, and his heart lifted. His beautiful wife sat under the shade of the oak tree in their backyard of a newly renovated home in Apple Creek. It was probably one of the last few warm days before the weather would turn cold and snowy.

Nick still couldn't believe they had been married almost a year now.

Major life decisions took on new meaning when time was no longer a luxury.

Mary Ruth sat on the blanket with Sarah. His mother-in-law sat in a lawn chair looking lovingly at her granddaughter in her daughter's arms.

Nick's heart nearly burst with joy.

Things could have gone far differently if God

hadn't been watching out for Sarah when Ruben had decided she was the root of his problems.

Turns out, Miss Ellinor, the pastor's wife, had confided in Ruben's mother about Sarah's need to get away from an abusive boyfriend. Her intentions had been innocent enough; Miss Ellinor was looking for a rental for Sarah. However, Ruben had eavesdropped. And when Mary Ruth had broken up with him, he used the information to try to scare Sarah. To make her think her ex had found her. Ruben had hoped to get Sarah away from Mary Ruth, whom he felt was unduly influenced by the evil *Englischer*.

Ruben confessed to everything, from throwing the rock through the church window to luring Sarah to the empty house and pushing her off the ladder. He never revealed whom he paid to make the phone call, but the young girl probably didn't realize what Ruben's true intentions were.

Thankfully, Ruben wasn't internet savvy, or he may have tracked down Jimmy himself and sent him after Sarah earlier. Nick prayed Ruben would change during his three-year stint in prison.

Nick needed to shove those memories aside, but he found they made him profoundly grateful.

He pushed open the back door and strolled across the lawn. "Hello. Did my little princess nap for you today?" He studied his wife's face.

She was tired, but she always assured him it was tired in the very best possible way.

Sarah shook her head and planted a kiss on her daughter's forehead. "I had help, though, so I was able to take a little nap." She handed their daughter over to Maggie and adjusted the blanket around the baby.

Sarah came to him and wrapped her arms around his waist. He cherished the easy nature of their relationship. Sarah took pleasure in the little things. She had been through so much and seemed to share in his feelings of gratitude. He kissed her forehead, impressed with how well the scar from the broken glass had healed.

A lot of scars had healed over the past year.

The baby let out a little cry and Sarah spun around, ready to take their daughter into her arms.

Maggie held up one hand. "I've got this under control. Did you forget who raised you?" Maggie smiled, her thin hair a soft halo around her head. She had defied all the doctors' expectations for life expectancy. Through both the Gardner women, Nick had learned to take each day as it came. Sarah's family was different from his, who were always looking for the next achievement. The next goal. The next honor.

Nick loved the family that he was born into, but he loved the contentedness and satisfaction he felt with his new family: Sarah and little Emma May.

Sarah reluctantly pulled out of Nick's embrace. Every time he came home from work—*every time* he entered a room—a flush of warm emotions wrapped around her heart.

Her life had been a nightmare when she first moved to Apple Creek; now it was more than she could have ever hoped. She glanced over her shoulder at her mother and Mary Ruth cooing over her fussing baby—*Nick's and her* baby.

"I better start dinner." Sarah moved toward the house.

"Oh, no, let me do it." Mary Ruth stood and swatted at the back of her long dress. Sarah waved her off.

"I enjoy cooking, especially if Emma May is content with her auntie Mary Ruth and Grammy."

Mary Ruth beamed. "I'm really going to miss you all."

A thin line creased Nick's brow. "Miss us?"

Mary Ruth shook her bonneted head. "I've decided to spend some time in Florida."

"Florida?" Nick asked, obviously only able to get one or two words out at a time.

Sarah placed her hand on her husband's forearm. "Mary Ruth is going to spend some time with her grandmother in an Amish community in Florida."

"It'll be a nice change of pace." Mary Ruth ran her hand down Emma May's soft head. "But I'll visit." She lifted a shoulder. "The community is in affiliation with Apple Creek. I'll be free to come back if I wish. I have to figure out what I want to do."

Marriage was a well-respected institution among the Amish, and it had become apparent that Mary Ruth felt alone among all her married or soon-to-be married friends.

"I've made some money selling my quilts to buy a bus ticket. I leave next week."

"Well," Nick said, "we'll miss you, too."

"Absolutely. Well…dinner isn't going to make itself." Sarah went into the kitchen and opened the refrigerator.

Nick came up behind her and wrapped his arms around her waist and nuzzled her neck. "You smell nice."

Sarah turned around in his embrace and hugged him back. "What did I ever do to deserve you?"

Nick whispered in her ear, "You've deserved only good things all along. I'm just glad I was here when you finally realized it."

* * * * *

Dear Reader,

I hope you enjoyed another trip to the Amish community of Apple Creek. This time, I told Sarah's story, an *Englischer*, who is forced to hide from her stalker ex-boyfriend among the Amish. But she doesn't simply hide—she uses her skills as a social worker to help the young people of the community, both Amish and non-Amish, who are struggling with everything from addiction to the stresses of adjusting to adult life.

When I first started researching the Amish, I was saddened to learn that even though they choose to live apart from the world, they are unable to escape some of the same issues, such as drugs and alcohol abuse, that are prevalent in the outside world. And in some ways, the struggle may be greater because of the extreme pressure to conform to the Amish way of life. I used this idea as a stepping-off point to plot *Plain Protector*.

I appreciate that you've taken the time to read my latest book. I'm happy to report that more books set in Apple Creek will be released in the near future. I hope you look for them. I keep an updated list of titles on my website: AlisonStone.com.

I love to hear from my readers. Please email me at Alison@AlisonStone.com or write to me at PO Box 333, Buffalo, NY 14051.

Live, Love, Laugh,

Alison Stone

LARGER-PRINT BOOKS!

GET 2 FREE
LARGER-PRINT NOVELS
PLUS 2 FREE
MYSTERY GIFTS

Love Inspired®

SUSPENSE
RIVETING INSPIRATIONAL ROMANCE

Larger-print novels are now available...

LARGER-PRINT BOOKS!

GET 2 FREE
LARGER-PRINT NOVELS
PLUS 2 FREE
MYSTERY GIFTS

Love Inspired®

Larger-print novels are now available...

YES! Please send me 2 FREE LARGER-PRINT Love Inspired® novels and my 2 FREE mystery gifts (gifts are worth about $10). After receiving them, if I don't wish to receive any more books, I can return the shipping statement marked "cancel." If I don't cancel, I will receive 6 brand-new novels every month and be billed just $5.49 per book in the U.S. or $5.99 per book in Canada. That's a savings of at least 19% off the cover price. It's quite a bargain! Shipping and handling is just 50¢ per book in the U.S. and 75¢ per book in Canada.* I understand that accepting the 2 free books and gifts places me under no obligation to buy anything. I can always return a shipment and cancel at any time. Even if I never buy another book, the two free books and gifts are mine to keep forever.

122/322 IDN GH6D

Name	(PLEASE PRINT)	
Address		Apt. #
City	State/Prov.	Zip/Postal Code

Signature (if under 18, a parent or guardian must sign)

Mail to the **Reader Service:**
IN U.S.A.: P.O. Box 1867, Buffalo, NY 14240-1867
IN CANADA: P.O. Box 609, Fort Erie, Ontario L2A 5X3

Are you a current subscriber to Love Inspired® books
and want to receive the larger-print edition?
Call 1-800-873-8635 or visit www.ReaderService.com.

* Terms and prices subject to change without notice. Prices do not include applicable taxes. Sales tax applicable in N.Y. Canadian residents will be charged applicable taxes. Offer not valid in Quebec. This offer is limited to one order per household. Not valid to current subscribers to Love Inspired Larger-Print books. All orders subject to credit approval. Credit or debit balances in a customer's account(s) may be offset by any other outstanding balance owed by or to the customer. Please allow 4 to 6 weeks for delivery. Offer available while quantities last.

Your Privacy—The Reader Service is committed to protecting your privacy. Our Privacy Policy is available online at www.ReaderService.com or upon request from the Reader Service.

We make a portion of our mailing list available to reputable third parties that offer products we believe may interest you. If you prefer that we not exchange your name with third parties, or if you wish to clarify or modify your communication preferences, please visit us at www.ReaderService.com/consumerchoice or write to us at Reader Service Preference Service, P.O. Box 9062, Buffalo, NY 14240-9062. Include your complete name and address.

LILP15

REQUEST YOUR FREE BOOKS!

2 FREE INSPIRATIONAL NOVELS
PLUS 2 *FREE* MYSTERY GIFTS

Love Inspired ® HISTORICAL

YES! Please send me 2 FREE Love Inspired® Historical novels and my 2 FREE mystery gifts (gifts are worth about $10). After receiving them, if I don't wish to receive any more books, I can return the shipping statement marked "cancel." If I don't cancel, I will receive 4 brand-new novels every month and be billed just $4.99 per book in the U.S. or $5.49 per book in Canada. That's a saving of at least 17% off the cover price. It's quite a bargain! Shipping and handling is just 50¢ per book in the U.S. and 75¢ per book in Canada.* I understand that accepting the 2 free books and gifts places me under no obligation to buy anything. I can always return a shipment and cancel at any time. Even if I never buy another book, the two free books and gifts are mine to keep forever.

102/302 IDN GH6Z

Name	(PLEASE PRINT)

Address	Apt. #

City	State/Prov.	Zip/Postal Code

Signature (if under 18, a parent or guardian must sign)

Mail to the **Reader Service:**
IN U.S.A.: P.O. Box 1867, Buffalo, NY 14240-1867
IN CANADA: P.O. Box 609, Fort Erie, Ontario L2A 5X3

Want to try two free books from another series?
Call 1-800-873-8635 or visit www.ReaderService.com.

* Terms and prices subject to change without notice. Prices do not include applicable taxes. Sales tax applicable in N.Y. Canadian residents will be charged applicable taxes. Offer not valid in Quebec. This offer is limited to one order per household. Not valid for current subscribers to Love Inspired Historical books. All orders subject to credit approval. Credit or debit balances in a customer's account(s) may be offset by any other outstanding balance owed by or to the customer. Please allow 4 to 6 weeks for delivery. Offer available while quantities last.

Your Privacy—The Reader Service is committed to protecting your privacy. Our Privacy Policy is available online at www.ReaderService.com or upon request from the Reader Service.

We make a portion of our mailing list available to reputable third parties that offer products we believe may interest you. If you prefer that we not exchange your name with third parties, or if you wish to clarify or modify your communication preferences, please visit us at www.ReaderService.com/consumerchoice or write to us at Reader Service Preference Service, P.O. Box 9062, Buffalo, NY 14240-9062. Include your complete name and address.

LIH15

REQUEST YOUR FREE BOOKS!
2 FREE WHOLESOME ROMANCE NOVELS
IN LARGER PRINT
PLUS 2
FREE
MYSTERY GIFTS

HEARTWARMING™

Wholesome, tender romances

YES! Please send me 2 FREE Harlequin® Heartwarming Larger-Print novels and my 2 FREE mystery gifts (gifts worth about $10). After receiving them, if I don't wish to receive any more books, I can return the shipping statement marked "cancel." If I don't cancel, I will receive 4 brand-new larger-print novels every month and be billed just $5.24 per book in the U.S. or $5.99 per book in Canada. That's a savings of at least 19% off the cover price. It's quite a bargain! Shipping and handling is just 50¢ per book in the U.S. and 75¢ per book in Canada.* I understand that accepting the 2 free books and gifts places me under no obligation to buy anything. I can always return a shipment and cancel at any time. Even if I never buy another book, the two free books and gifts are mine to keep forever.

161/361 IDN GHX2

Name   (PLEASE PRINT)

Address   Apt. #

City   State/Prov.   Zip/Postal Code

Signature (if under 18, a parent or guardian must sign)

Mail to the **Reader Service:**
IN U.S.A.: P.O. Box 1867, Buffalo, NY 14240-1867
IN CANADA: P.O. Box 609, Fort Erie, Ontario L2A 5X3

* Terms and prices subject to change without notice. Prices do not include applicable taxes. Sales tax applicable in N.Y. Canadian residents will be charged applicable taxes. Offer not valid in Quebec. This offer is limited to one order per household. Not valid for current subscribers to Harlequin Heartwarming larger-print books. All orders subject to credit approval. Credit or debit balances in a customer's account(s) may be offset by any other outstanding balance owed by or to the customer. Please allow 4 to 6 weeks for delivery. Offer available while quantities last.

Your Privacy—The Reader Service is committed to protecting your privacy. Our Privacy Policy is available online at www.ReaderService.com or upon request from the Reader Service.

We make a portion of our mailing list available to reputable third parties that offer products we believe may interest you. If you prefer that we not exchange your name with third parties, or if you wish to clarify or modify your communication preferences, please visit us at www.ReaderService.com/consumerchoice or write to us at Reader Service Preference Service, P.O. Box 9062, Buffalo, NY 14240-9062. Include your complete name and address.

HW15